Mates, Dates Guide

To Life, Love, and

Looking Luscious

Mates, Dates Guide To Life, Love, and Looking Luscious

Cathy Hopkins

Simon Pulse

New York   London   Toronto   Sydney

This book is a work of fiction. Any references to historical events,
real people, or real locales are used fictitiously. Other names, characters,
places, and incidents are the product of the author's imagination,
and any resemblance to actual events or locales or persons,
living or dead, is entirely coincidental.

SIMON PULSE
An imprint of Simon & Schuster Children's Publishing Division
1230 Avenue of the Americas, New York, NY 10020
Text copyright © 2005 by Cathy Hopkins
Illustrations copyright © 2005 by Sue Hellard
Originally published in Great Britain in 2005 by Piccadilly Press Ltd.
Published by arrangement with Piccadilly Press Ltd.
All rights reserved, including the right of reproduction
in whole or in part in any form.
SIMON PULSE and colophon are registered trademarks
of Simon & Schuster, Inc.

Designed by Debra Sfetsios
The text of this book was set in Bembo.

Manufactured in the United States of America
First Simon Pulse edition June 2005

2 4 6 8 10 9 7 5 3 1

Library of Congress Control Number 2004118123

ISBN 1-4169-0279-1

Mates, Dates Guide To Life, Love, and Looking Luscious

 # Contents

PART ONE: Boys and Relationships

PART TWO: Beauty, Health, and Fashion

PART THREE: Survival Tips for Every Occasion

PART FOUR: Relaxation and Fun Time

PART FIVE: Riding the Roller Coaster

A Note From Us

Hi, everyone.

First we'd like to say how totally top it is that we—"we" being Izzie, Lucy, Nesta, and TJ— have been asked to put this book together. We hope you enjoy our efforts. It's certainly been a blast doing it.

If you look in our contents list, you'll see that we've tried to put in something for everyone and just about everybody we know has chipped in somewhere along the line.

There are fashion tips from Lucy, tips on boys and relationships from Nesta and her brother Tony who, as some of you who have read any of the Mates, Dates series will know, fancies himself as the Master Snogger. (Lucy says he's not bad at it either.) Izzie's contributed with all she knows about natural remedies and all the New Agey stuff she's into—including a section on spells for pulling boys when all else has failed. There's advice from TJ about being streetwise and making the best of where you live. TJ's mum, Dr. Watts, came through with anything medical, Lucy's dad with advice about nutrition, Cressida Forbes on social etiquette and we even roped in Lucy's brothers, Steve and Lal. We weren't too sure about Lal's contributions, but had to give in when he threatened to put embarrassing photos of Lucy when she was five years old on the internet. He really has a lot to learn about the subtler techniques for getting his way with girls.

For anyone who hasn't read any of the Mates, Dates books, we thought it was a good idea to start this guide with an introduction to who we are. Not because we're swanky big-heads or anything, but so that you know who's who.

A big thank you to all the contributors and hope you fabtastic readers out there enjoy the book.

Luv, peace, and chocolate.
Rock on.
Izzie, Lucy, Nesta, and TJ.

Note from Nesta: Personally, I'd have edited out Cressida Forbes bit (and anyone who's read *Mates, Dates, and Designer Divas* will know exactly why—she is a snotty cow), but this is a team effort and the others wanted her bit in.

Profiles

Izzie

Name: Izzie Foster.

Star sign: Aquarius.

Age: Fifteen.

Height: Five foot eight inches and still growing in all directions and I can tell you, it's *not* funny!

Hair color: Chestnut at the moment, but once I dyed it green (didn't go down too well at the time as I was bridesmaid at my stepsister's wedding and she wasn't well pleased!)

Eye color: Green. To match my hair. Sometimes.

Race: Egg and spoon. Haha. Oh, I see. British (cue reggae version of "God Save the Queen").

How would you describe yourself in three words? I found this hard to do, so I asked the girls. They said, weird (blooming cheek), rebellious (also blooming cheek) and wise (okay, that bit's cool, although totally inaccurate)

Where were you born? Hampstead, London, England.

Where do you live? Finchley, North London.

Who do you live with? My mum and my stepdad, Angus. I

used to call him the Lodger as I wasn't v. keen on him in the beginning, but it's cool now.

Parents' occupations: Dad lectures in English literature at a university in town (he's remarried with a little boy and lives not far away, in Primrose Hill), Mum's an accountant, Angus is an accountant (how dull is that?).

Worst moment of your life: When my dad left. And watching any news about wars and people being killed. It makes me feel *really* depressed.

Best moment of your life: The first time I sang with the band King Noz.

Pin up? What? My skirt? Dad says it's short enough.

What couldn't you live without? My mates: Lucy, Nesta and TJ.

What is the most important thing that life has taught you? That boys may come and go, but friends are forever.

What would you most like to change about yourself? My expanding bum. It's expanding at twice the rate of the universe. As our neighbour, Mrs. Schneider, would say, enough already.

What makes you laugh? Lucy's daft jokes.

Fave book: *Junk* by Melvin Burgess.

What do you do to cheer yourself up? Spend time with

my mates. And a hot chocolate with marshmallow melts doesn't hurt either. No wonder my bum is big!

What's your best subject at school? Music.

Fave food: Broccoli. Oh okay, if I'm honest, chocolate.

Fave color: Silver.

Fave movie: *The Seven Faces of Dr. Lao.* It was made yonks ago in 1964, but it's still really cool.

Interests: Music. Movies. Anything new age. Witchcraft (reading about it, not practising).

Talents: Singing (so I'm told).

Goals: To write and sing my own lyrics and to travel the world.

Something secret about you: Ah, but then it wouldn't be secret! okay, once when I was grounded for a few days, I practised snogging on the back of my hand. (Arghhhh, how embarrassing.)

Lucy

Name: Lucy Lovering.

Star sign: Gemini (sign of the twins or the schizophrenic. No it isn't. Yes it is).

Age: Fifteen.

Height: I don't like to talk about my height (or lack of it). Let it be said that I am petite.

Hair color: Blond.

Eye color: Blue.

Race: Half-English, half-Scottish, or possibly alien.

How would you describe yourself in 3 words? I also found this hard to do, so I asked the girls. They said, sweet (yuck), gentle and funny.

Where were you born? North London, planet earth, the universe.

Where do you live? East Finchley/Muswell Hill border. Planet earth, the . . . etc.

Who do you live with? Mum, Dad, older brothers Steve and Lal, Labrador dogs Ben and Jerry.

Parents' occupations: Mum's a counselor, Dad runs a health food store and teaches guitar in the evenings.

Worst moment of your life: After a disastrous haircut, my mates took me shopping for a Wonderbra to cheer me up and even in the titchiest one, I still looked like I was wearing my mum's bra. And, like Izzie, any bad news on the telly about people blowing each other up. I really, *really* wish we could all live in peace on this planet.

Best moment of your life: Oh God. There are loads. Um. Any time spent with my mates (and I'm not sucking up either, I really mean it). And the first time Nesta's brother Tony kissed me. It was awesome.

Pin up? Keeps changing. Though Orlando Bloom is my current cutie.

What couldn't you live without? Air (hahahaha).

What is the most important thing that life has taught you? That everything changes. One day it may feel like you're life is over, but it can all change, sometimes in twenty-four hours.

What would you most like to change about yourself? I'd like boobs that don't look like pinpricks.

What makes you laugh? My boobs. No really. Er. Mike Myers's movies.

Fave book: I still like the Narnia books by C. S. Lewis. I'd like to meet Aslan.

What do you do to cheer yourself up? Spend time with mates.

What's your best subject at school? Art.

Fave food: Ben & Jerry's Chunky Monkey ice cream.

Fave color: Blue (sort of turquoise blue).

Fave movie: *Sleepless in Seattle.* It's so romantic.

Interests: Dressmaking, fashion, music, movies.

Talents: Dressmaking, art.

Goals: To have my own dress label called LL (Lucy Lovering designs) and do all the big fashion events to International acclaim.

Something secret about you: I was going to put a secret about Tony but he might read this so I'm not going to.

Nesta

Name: Nesta Williams.

Star sign: Leo.

Age: Fifteen.

Height: Five foot seven inches.

Hair color: Black.

Eye color: Brown.

Race: Half-Jamaican, half-Italian and a bit of Spanish thrown in there too, *ole ole ole olay.*

How would you describe yourself in three words: I too found this hard to do, so I asked the girls. They said, dramatic (*moi?* As if!), colorful (meaning what?) and fun (cool).

Where were you born? Bristol, England.

Where do you live? Highgate, North London.

Who do you live with? Mum, Dad, and half-brother Tony.

Parents' occupations: Dad's a film/TV director, Mum works as a news presenter on cable TV.

Worst moment of your life: When my mates weren't speaking to me after Izzie's first gig and I ran off and had to make my own way home late at night and it was really scary as there were weird people about and I felt sick. And I also found changing schools pretty awful at first, but then I got in with Izzie, Lucy, and later TJ, so it was okay.

Best moment of your life: There have been a few. No, actually, a load. The dressing-up and anticipation before a first date. The build-up and anticipation before a first kiss. Having a laugh with my mates when the first date and first kiss go AWOL. Hey ho and on we go. Oh, and getting home one night after stupidly making my own way home after one of Izzie's gigs (see **Worst moment**), Dad coming out of the sitting room so I knew I was home safe. I was *sooo* happy to be home. Sadly, then I threw up all over the hall floor. It's one way of saying hi.

Pin up? Ah. So many boys, so little time. Brad. Enrique, Orlando. How long have you got?

What couldn't you live without? My mates. My Wonderbra. My lip-gloss. My hairdryer. My mobile.

What is the most important thing that life has taught you? That before you criticise someone, walk a mile in their shoes. That way, you are a mile away from them. *And* you have their shoes. Hahaha.

What would you most like to change about yourself? My big feet (size nine). And my big mouth as I keep putting my big feet in it.

What makes you laugh? The problem pages in teen mags.

Fave book: Does *Hello* magazine count?

What do you do to cheer yourself up? Spend time with my mates.

What's your best subject at school? Drama, dahhling luvvie.

Fave food: Potato wedges and sour cream.

Fave color: To wear: black. On the wall: lavender. Just as a color: sky blue.

Fave movie: *Breakfast at Tiffany's*. Audrey Hepburn is so stylish.

Interests: Boys. Movies. Fashion. Boys.

Talents: Acting. Pulling boys.

Goals: To be a famous actress.

Something secret about you: Sometimes I think awful things about strangers. Like someone gets on the tube and before I can control it, my mind says, Ooo, there goes an ugly one. Then I feel dead rotten. They can't help it. (Please don't tell anyone.)

TJ

Name: TJ Watts.

Star sign: Sagittarius (sign of the archer, half man, half horse. Erk!).

Age: Fifteen.

Height: Five foot seven inches.

Hair color: Brown.

Eye color: Brown. Conker brown to be precise.

Race: *Anglaise.*

How would you describe yourself in three words: A good mate (I hope).

Where were you born? Muswell Hill, London, England.

Where do you live? Muswell Hill, North London.

Who do you live with? Mum and Dad (I call them "the wrinklies" because they're really old). My dog, Mojo. And sometimes my brother, Paul, when he's not off travelling the world. I have a sister too (Marie), but she's married now and lives in Devon.

Parents' occupations: Both doctors. Dad's a hospital consultant, Mum runs a general practice.

Worst moment of your life: When my mate Hannah left to live in South Africa.

Best moment of your life: When I realized that Lucy,

Nesta, and Izzie were serious about being my new mates.

Pin up? Albert Einstein. I wouldn't want to snog him, though.

What couldn't you live without? Nesta, Lucy, Izzie, and Mojo.

What is the most important thing that life has taught you? That trust is the most important thing in a friendship and to be totally honest with your mates.

What would you most like to change about yourself? I'd like to be able to act cooler when I meet boys I like as sometimes I turn into Noola the Alien girl and talk Outerspaceagongalese.

What makes you laugh? The movies *Wayne's World*, 1 and 2.

Fave book: *The Curious Incident of the Dog in the Night-time* by Mark Haddon.

What do you do to cheer yourself up? Spend time with my mates. Oh God. I've just seen that we've all written that. Oh well. It's true.

What's your best subject at school? English.

Fave food: Chips. The big chunky kind.

Fave color: Violet.

Fave movie: *Sense and Sensibility*, based on the book by Jane Austen, starring Emma Thompson and Kate Winslet. I was *totally* in love with Greg Wise who played Willoughby (even though he was a love rat).

Interests: Books, history, writing, boys, music, movies, travel, documentaries.

Talents: Um. Writing.

Goals: To write novels.

Something secret about you: Sometimes I do still think about a boy called Luke De Biasi and feel a bit sad that things didn't work out for us.

Other Contributors:

Tony Williams (Nesta's brother)

Steve Lovering (Lucy's brother)

Lal Lovering (Lucy's brother)

Mrs. Foster (Izzie's mum)

Mrs. Lovering (Lucy's mum)

Mr. Lovering (Lucy's dad)

Mrs. Allen (our headmistress)

Cressida Forbes (friend of Simon Peddington Lee, who is
    Nesta's ex-boyfriend)

Dr. Watts (TJ's mum)

Assorted boys: Ben Taylor, Mark Boden, Luke De Biasi,
Steve and Lal's classmates.

And Ben and Jerry didn't want to be left out so here's their
contribution:

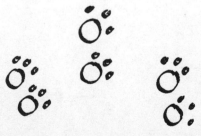

Part One
Boys and Relationships

by Nesta Williams

Boys

planet "boy"

Starting with none other than one of our favorite subjects, *le garçon, il ragazzo*, that mysterious species of aliens—boys.

Where to Find Them

Some girls, especially at single-sex schools, say things like, "Oh, we never meet boys. There aren't any around. There's a shortage." Not true. They're everywhere. After extensive (and totally enjoyable!) research, these are our top ten best places to find them:

1. Sports centres. Usually showing off, but then that is what boys like to do.

2. Music stores. A lot of boys tend to be more anoraky than girls when it comes to music and loads of them like to fantasise about being the next big thing to hit the charts. Anyway, you can act all girlie and ask for a recommendation as boys love to (again) show off their superior knowledge. However, if you decide to take this line, be prepared to listen to an hour-long lecture on the life and times of some obscure band from the Sixties. Listening does work, though, because everyone likes to be asked what their opinion is. Whilst he's giving you his, try to perfect your "oh, how fascinating" look which is a cross between glee and constipation. (At least it is when Lucy does it.)

3. Coming out of school. What better way to check out a whole selection? This is where Lucy first spotted Tony before she knew he was Nesta's brother and it was lurve at first sight.

4. At discos or clubs. Usually they're with their mates in these places, though, and boys tend to act differently when they're out in a group. If you fancy one, try and get him on his own to get a better idea of what he's like.

5. Through mates. Most mates

have a brother. And that brother has mates. And those mates have mates. And so . . . you get the picture. (Sadly none of us fancy any of Steve and Lal's mates or Tony's, but, you never know, one day one of them might bring home a cutenik.)

6. At night classes or school clubs. Loads of boys do extra classes, but it might mean that you end up doing a class in boxing or car mechanics or something. No problem, as it doesn't hurt to learn some of these things.

7. At the cinema (hanging out before or after the movie).

8. At gigs and rock concerts.

9. At the mall whilst shopping—though it might take some explaining at to why you hang around in the men's department. You could say that you're shopping for your brother and once again, need advice on what label is best, etc . . .

10. At parties. This is a top place for meeting new boys as you get to dress up, so you will inevitably be looking your best.

Other places are: cafés, football matches, bowling alleys (especially if boys are in the next lane), swimming pools, ice-skating rinks in winter (as you get to hold hands), out walking the dog (it helps if you have one of your own, by the way), sunbathing in the park or on the beach in summer. Basically, you're not going to meet anyone if you don't get out there.

Funny enough, though, often you meet boys when you're not looking for one. And not so funny enough, on days when your hair needs washing, you haven't got a scrap of makeup on and were least expecting to run in to Mr. Gorgie Pants. All you can do then is smile. As Lucy's mum is always saying, it's the most important thing you wear!

What did Cinderella say when her photographs didn't arrive back from processing? Some day my prints will come.

What Boys Want

The Bad News: According to a recent survey (Tony, Ben, Steve, Lal, Mark, Luke and all the boys we could find at local schools), it was found that top of most boys' lists of what they want in a girl is good looks, whereas most girls look for a sense of humour. Let's face it, we need one for when we meet the boys. Haha. But seriously, some wise person (Lucy's mum again) said that a male is seduced through his eyes whereas a female is seduced through her ears, i.e. through what boys say, not by them sticking anything into your ears. Yurgh.

Anyway, the first thing that hits boys is how you look. You may have a stunning personality, be the kindest person ever, but tough, because for that all important *first* impression, he's looking at your face, your body or your legs.

The Good News: In this day and age, anyone, even the plainest Jane can look like a top babe. If you don't believe us then you get homework.

Homework For Non-believers

- Go to video/DVD rental store.
- Check the store for boys, as getting out DVDs can also be a good place to meet the opposite sex and you can do your "Oh, can you recommend something?" routine again.
- Take out two videos—*Being John Malkovich* and *The Mask*, both starring Cameron Diaz.
- Go home and watch.

You will see that in *Being John Malkovich*, Cameron Diaz looks a right frumpette, complete with frizzy hair. In *The Mask,* she looks like a five-star babe. Same girl. Different hair, different clothes.

The lesson to be learned from this homework is that with the right hair, products and clothes, *everyone*—and I mean everyone—can be made to look good. It only takes a bit of effort. If you're one of these girls who thinks, No way I'm going to dress up for some stupid boy—I want someone to like me hairy legs and all, I'm a free spirit, blah blah. . . . Fine. We wish you luck.

For those of you who want to look good, the

world and pick of the boys is yours (see Lucy's top tips on making the most of yourself in the Beauty, Fashion and Health section)

Here's what our survey revealed:

☆ What Boys Say They Want ☆

1. Good looks
2. Confidence
3. Enthusiasm (no one wants to hang out with a party pooper)
4. Intelligence
5. Sense of humour
6. Patience and warmth
7. Generosity
   (It goes downhill from here.)
8. Great boobs (that's me out—Lucy)
9. Great legs (And that's me out. I have lumpy knees—Izzie)
10. A great ass (Pff. How scientific is this survey anyway?—TJ)

Those are the qualities that the boys said they wanted. (Take it with a pinch of salt. We did. . . . And a sock in the mouth!)

More On What Boys Want

Tony: A *Vogue* model with an IQ of a hundred and forty-five who has eyes only for me.

Steve: An intelligent girl I can have a good conversation with.

Lal: A girl who adores me and who is about a metre tall with a flat head so I can rest my Coke can on her. No. Actually the truth is, most girls don't realize the power that they have just by simply being *female*. Most boys I know just want to pull and all girls have the right equipment! You don't have to be skinny or look like some magazine model. A bit of girlie stuff like smelling nice, shiny hair, lip gloss and a good sense of humour and we're happy believe me. You don't have to be a babe. We're knocked out just by the fact you have curvy bits.

Luke De Biasi: A cross between Madame Curie and Jessica Rabbit will do me.

okay, enough boys. We get the picture.

What Boys Don't Want

NO

✘ Smelly (as if! But seriously boys do like girls who smell nice).

✘ Girls who swear. Surprising, this one. They can swear their heads off, but a lot of boys don't like girls who do.

✘ Too "in your face" and demanding.

✘ Loud.

✘ Complicated (Ever met a girl who wasn't? It's part of our mysterious allure).

✘ Depressed.

✘ Whingey/whiney.

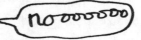

noooooo

✘ Out of control.

✘ Girls who go on about their ex-boyfriends.

✘ Girls who are always on a diet.

✘ Girls who keep moaning on about bits of their body that they don't like. One boy said, he particularly didn't like girls who complain about their big bums. He said, the bigger the better, as far as he was concerned. (Hurrah. Give me his number—Izzie.)

✘ Girls who need to dissect every stage of the relationship

no....

("We need to talk" seem to be the four words most boys dread).

✘ Girls who use four letter words (such as "don't," "stop," or "love").

✘ Girls who don't know how to have a good time.

✘ Girls who don't contribute to the conversation.

✘ Girls who play too many mind games.

It is important to find a boy who is always willing to
  help in times of trouble.
It is important to find a boy who makes you laugh when
  you're feeling blue.
It is important to find a boy who is depend-
    able and doesn't lie.
It is important to find a boy who
    is a good kisser.
It is important that these four boys
    never meet!

Types of Boys

Some girls think that there are only two types of boys. The ones you want and the ones you get. Of course that's not true. Boys come in different shapes and sizes with different personalities—nice guys, rats, DIY boys, trainspotters, music buffs, brainboxes, boy-scout types, sporty, computer whizzes, diplomats, dreamers, poets, romantics, heroes, athletes, bullies, adventurers, Casanovas, slimeballs, geeks, babe magnets . . .

The list is endless and some boys can be a mixture, i.e. you can meet an athletic Casanova or an academic Casanova. Basically, there are all sorts out there.

What's the difference between a snowman and a snowwoman? Snowballs.

How to Get Noticed

So . . . how do you get noticed?

Immediate:

- Trip over him (some boys are wise to this ploy, but if he likes what he sees, he'll be flattered.)
- Position yourself so that he trips over you.
- Position yourself in his line of vision and make eye contact.
- Position yourself in his line of vision and flirt outrageously with someone else. (Not with one of your girl friends or your dad!)
- At a party, offer to take round the food and drink, that way you'll have a natural excuse to get chatting.
- Say you're writing a book like this one and are doing a survey on what boys want, etc. We found it was a great way to get chatting to loads of boys. Make sure you take your notepad and pen with you so that it looks genuine.

Planning Ahead:

- Do your homework: find out all about him and what he's into from mutual friends. Then next time you meet him, reveal your knowledge about his interest while chatting and he'll be astounded at how well-informed you are.

- Solicit help. Get mutual friends to arrange an outing or throw a party and invite both of you.

- Find out where he goes to school, then accidentally bump into him outside one day.

- Find out where he likes to hang out, e.g. what gym/video store he goes to. Again, an "accidental" meeting. Remember life helps those who help themselves.

- Find out his interests and get involved (unless, of course, his interest happens to be someone called Sara. Or Tarquin . . .)

Another Way of Getting Noticed:

Dance naked in his back garden. (Okay, not such a great idea—at least not in winter.)

> She: How strange! You look just like my fifth boyfriend.
> He: Fifth! Why how many have you had?
> She: Four.

Nesta's Top Tips on Getting Noticed

- Be blindingly beautiful. There's no such thing as a plain girl, only one who can't be bothered. With some lippie, good sunglasses, clean, shiny hair, anyone can be a babe.
- Smile and make direct eye contact.
- Spray yourself with your fave perfume (don't overdo it, though), then walk past so he gets a hint of a gorgeous scent, or approach him, lean in close, and ask if you can borrow a pen.
- Wear heels to make your legs look long and fab.
- Get a Wonderbra and boy, will you get noticed.
- Stand up straight. Don't

hello boys!

slouch. It's the first thing they teach at model school. Good posture makes you look more confident and makes your body look slimmer.

Lucy's Tips

- Pray for a miracle.
- Grow another six inches so they don't miss you in the crowd.

Izzie's Tips

- Relax around them. Boys hate desperate girls.
- Make eye contact, then smile.

- Laugh at his jokes.

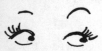

- Don't be too available. Play hard to get for a while because most boys like a challenge.

TJ's Tips

- Be confident. Don't whinge on about what you don't like about yourself.
- Flirt outrageously, then go home. It will leave him wanting more.
- Don't smoke as it will make your hair and your breath stink.

As you smoke, so shall you reek

So once you've got him to notice you, then what? Different approaches work for different boys. Here are some tried and tested ideas—according to all the girls we interviewed at our school. Take your pick but note some work better than others.

Techniques for Different Boys

1. *The "Be Yourself" Technique (for straightforward boys)*
- Be yourself. Your best self, that is. Not your "I've got PMT and am having a lousy day" self.
- Don't try to copy anyone else.
- The best become the best by being themselves.

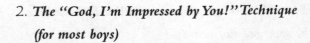

(We like this approach best.)

2. *The "God, I'm Impressed by You!" Technique (for most boys)*

- Act attentive, fascinated by his every word.
- Lots of enthusiastic body language, (leaning forward, nodding, exclaiming)
- Use lots of eye contact.
- Laugh at all his jokes (even the crapola ones)
- Act as though he's telling you something you didn't know. (Flattery gets you everywhere.)

3. **The "Mummy Therapist" Technique (for little boys at heart)**
- Make him feel safe and understood.
- Invite him home and feed him comfort foods.
- Listen to him.
- Encourage him.
- Give him little treats.
- Don't judge him.
- Only see the best in him.

(This can work brilliantly and is very popular, but it can backfire if you're not really a motherly type. You can start to resent the fact that what you presented in the first place is what he's grown to expect—and who can blame him!)

4. **The "Doormat" Technique (for bossy, bully boys who like girls to be seen and not heard)**

- Get a T-shirt with "Welcome! Wipe Your Feet On Me" written on it.
- Always let him have his way.
- Serve his every whim.
- Never complain.
- Tell him he's wonderful at every opportunity.
- Dress exactly the way that pleases him the most regardless of what you like.
- Stop seeing your friends if he doesn't like them.

(You might think that it's a joke, but sadly, some girls actually do this. We wouldn't recommend it as relationships are a two-way street and both parties have to have their say.)

5. *The "Seductress-Femme-Fatale" Technique*
- Dress in exquisitely tasteful and expensive-looking clothes that say, "I only want (and get) the best."
- Speak in a low soft voice.
- Toss your hair back from your face.
- Wear wonderful perfume, have dark nails and high heels.
- Have a graceful dignified walk and posture.
- Perfect the fleeting come-hither look.

- Do long languid body postures like a panther in repose.
- Home in on your target and make him feel special, like he's the only boy in the room.
- Make lots of innuendoes and make extended eye contact.

(Note from Nesta: This is one of my favorites.)

6. *The "One of the Lads" Technique (for boys who say they don't want a girlfriend)*

- Become good friends, swap jokes.
- Look after him.
- Don't flirt with or touch him.
- Be casual, get involved in his interests.
- Win his trust and build his confidence.
- Let him know that you don't want anything from him.

(When he feels safe with you, remind him that you're a girl by turning up dressed like a hot babe—or else, because he's feeling good about girls, he'll go off with the next one he meets and won't look back for a sec, since you weren't really into having a relationship with him, were you? You were just friends, right?)

7. The "Challenge" (for boys who don't like it too easy)

- Play hard to get.
- Flirt outrageously, but maintain unavailability.
- Be in control. Disagree intelligently and back up your arguments.
- Observe his answers quietly with a look of amused disdain.
- Practise cheeky lines like Mae West's: "Come and see me sometime" or "Come up Wednesday—that's amateur night."

(Some boys feel that if something or someone is worth having, they have to work for it—so let them.)

8. The "Little-Princess-Girlie" Technique (for boys who like to feel big and strong)

- Let him know that you need help—like with a plug or carrying your homework.
- Perfect the wide-eyed, innocent, vulnerable look.
- Wear little girlie clothes (flowery, ribbons etc.)

- Learn to wobble your bottom lip as if you're about to cry in times of crisis and lisp a little—"If thomeone doethn't thort this all out thoon . . ."
- Praise him emphatically when he does anything for you.

(This works well for boys who like girls to be childlike so that they can feel big and strong. We have three words to say for girls who use this technique and those are: "Get a life.")

Top Tips on the Art of Flirting

Do:

✔ Relax and be yourself.

✔ Be confident.

✔ Make fleeting body contact like brushing his hand when you pass something to him. Touch his arm when he says something funny.

✔ Smile.

✔ Mirror his body language.

✔ Laugh at his jokes, no matter how bad they are.

✔ Listen to what he has to say and look interested—fascinated, even. Ask him lots of questions to show you're really interested in him.

✔ Look into his eyes and maintain contact a moment too long to show that you're interested. Then look away.

✔ Lean slightly towards him while you're chatting.

✔ Flatter specific attributes. Everyone secretly knows what their good points are, so it always feels fab when other people notice too. So look for them—nice mouth, nice eyes, great hair. If you go in with a general line, he might think you say it to everyone. However, if you notice what is unique about him and compliment that, he'll think you're on the level and really have noticed him.

✔ Make him feel special and pay attention to him by focusing on what he's saying. Don't look round the room or over his shoulder to see if there's anyone better on offer.

✔ Keep it fun, be charming. Keep conversations light and casual, so learn how to small talk. Chat about situations you both have in common or something that's currently happening—latest movies, how do you know so and so? That sort of thing.

Right: Hi. Have you tried the tortilla dip? It's fab.

Wrong: Hi. I'm staying away from that tortilla dip as I'm on a diet and anyway, I'm feeling rotten tonight. I blame my parents. They split up when I was young so you'll probably dump me—that is, if you even go out with me in the first place. I've always felt like I'm a loser. Hey, let me tell you all about it. . . . (Exit boy.)

✔ Leave him wanting more so don't overstay your welcome. Just as things are going great, say at a party, say, "Okay, must go and circulate now." He'll think, "Hey, she was fun," and probably seek you out later.

✔ Soften your voice.

✔ Practice flirting with everyone as practice makes perfect. It will show you how easy it is, will quickly become second nature to you and build your confidence.

Don't:

✘ Always wait for him to make the move or come up with an opening line.

✘ Go on about other boyfriends.

✘ Be too easy or available.

✘ Act desperate.

✘ Be clingy.

✘ Get heavy, serious or too emotional. Something mega dramatic might be happening in your life, but if you go on about it too much in the early stages, he might think,

Woah, drama queen, high maintenance, I'm outta here.

✗ Stand too close and crowd his space.

✗ Brag. (Get a friend to brag about you on your behalf that way, you look wonderful. And modest!)

✗ Only wait to flirt with boys you fancy. You'll get rusty.

NB: To check if a boy is interested: Make eye contact a moment too long (as mentioned before). Move and hide behind a pillar or wall where you can see him, but he can't see you. Watch to see if he looks to where you were last standing and on seeing you gone, looks round for you. If he does, he's interested.

What's the definition of a flirt?
A girl who thinks it's every
man for herself.

Reading Body Language

- Dilated pupils are sometimes a clue that he's interested. Sadly, they can also mean that he's out of his head on something!

- Extended eye contact can mean he's attracted to you. It can also mean that he's shortsighted and trying to work out if he fancies you or if you're his sister.

- Leaning towards you or in on you can mean that he wants to be near you. It can also mean that he's had too much to drink!

- Mirroring your posture or hand signals is always a good sign as it means that he is empathising with you.

NB: Sometimes it almost impossible to read a boy's body language. In fact, he may act as if he dislikes you when in actual fact, he fancies you like mad. Boys fear rejection and it can feel scary to really like someone, so some boys go totally the other way and act cool and disinterested even though they like that person. If you really like the boy, give him a chance to get over being cool by being encouraging. Give him a signal that you like him and you'll soon see his body language change!

Meeting The One

Some people believe in the romantic notion that somewhere out there is a very special person just for them. The One. Your soul mate. Someone who you'll recognise because you feel at your best with him, and you'll feel you were destined to be with them. We had varying opinions on this, but really it's up to you if you if you choose to believe in "The One" theory or not.

Nesta: Who says you only get One? If you're lucky, you will meet The One, The Two, The Three . . . and so on.

Lucy: Don't put off seeing other boys or waste too much time waiting for The One in case he lives in Outer Mongolia and never travels. If you do meet him, you will know him at once and can take it from there.

Izzie: If it's meant to be, destiny will bring you together in this life as it has in past lives.

TJ: It's all chemical. The One is just a way of saying you fancy someone and your pheromones are mutually attractive.

How to Spot a Rat

Basically, he doesn't phone when he says he will. Is totally unreliable. He lies. He's late. He's vague about what he does when he's not with you. He doesn't listen to you or looks bored or amused when you're pouring out your heart. He cheats. He doesn't respect you.

Don't get involved.

Trouble is, sometimes even the smartest of girls doesn't realize that a boy is a rat until too late. This is because often a rat looks exactly the same as a nice guy. (Both TJ and I got fooled into falling for the same love rat once and he really seemed like a nice guy at first. It almost broke our friendship up until we realized that being mates was more important than being with a boy we couldn't trust.)

As with their body language, sometimes boys are hard to read. Hard to understand. Which brings me to our next section.

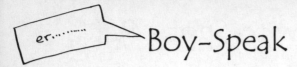

Boy-Speak

What He Says	What He Means
Call you later.	*. . . if I remember and even then probably not for a week or so. (And remember, a watched phone never rings.)*
Commitment.	*Usually only applies to a football team.*
I need space.	*. . . for my other girlfriends.*
Let's just see how it goes	*Back off, I'm feeling pressured.*
Would you like a back rub?	*I want to grope you.*
Isn't it warm in here?	*I want to grope you and am hoping you'll take your clothes off.*
Hi. Your friend looks nice.	*I fancy her and I'm using you to get to her.*
Don't get heavy.	*I don't feel the same way about you.*
She's ugly / a lesbian.	*She didn't fancy me.*

I'm not ready for a relationship.	*. . . at least not with you.*
I'm very independent.	*I like my own way.*
I think we should be free to date other people.	*I already am.*
We can still be friends.	*You're history, baby.*

So you've got him to notice you. He's got your number. Then what?

The general rule is that if a boy is interested, you don't have to wonder if he'll call or not. He will. In his own time, but he will.

Of course there are exceptions:

1 He's shy.
2. He's lost your number.
3. He put your number in his jeans pocket and those jeans went in the wash.
4. He's lazy.
5. He might fear rejection.

It can be hard for boys to do the all the running and asking for a date can be scary. In which case, *you* could always ask *him*. But remember . . .

- Pick your time. Ask him when he's on his own as sometimes boys act too cool or embarrassed when with their mates.
- Give at least a few days' notice—if you ask him out for that night, he may be busy. However, if he is busy but interested, he will probably say something like, "Oh sorry, I can't make tonight, but how about another time?" If turning you down, he won't give an opening for another time or will make an excuse. A genuine excuse is usually backed up with an alternative arrangement.
- Be cool about it. Don't declare undying love and tell him you've been watching him for weeks. He might think, Whoa! Stalker!
- Be confident. Don't start your invite by saying, "I don't suppose . . ." Be positive. Say, "Would you like to . . . ?"
- If you think he might not be ready for a one-to-one date, you could ask him to join you with a bunch of mates.

Keep it casual, like there's a bunch of us going to a con-
cert on Saturday, like to join us? Or invite him to a party
as you can say we need some extra boys.

- If he declines and doesn't offer an alternative date, move on.

But say he does call. He asks you out on a date. Fantastic.
What *then*?

Dating
First Dates

Do:

✔ Be cool and not too over
  eager if asked out, but do show
  that you're pleased.

Right:

He: Let's get together some time.

You: (big smile) Sure. Sounds good.

He: How about next Friday?

Wrong:

He: Let's get together some time.

You: Yes. Hold on, I'll get my diary. I'm free tonight or I could come over right now.

He: Um. I'll call you.

✔ Be encouraging as it probably took the boy a lot of nerve to get the courage up to ask you. (Unless you're Tony, who is under the impression that all girls are gagging to go out with him. Not all boys are as confident as he is.)

✔ Make some effort, but don't go over the top. Dress so that you look good, but are comfortable in what you're wearing—but not too comfortable, like in your pajamas.

✔ Offer to pay your way. Usually whoever has asked you on a date should pay the first time, but don't assume. Offer to go "Dutch" and pay your share. He can always refuse to let you.

✔ If he pays you a compliment, take it. Say thank you. Don't go into a whole thing about how short/fat/ugly you really are as a) it sounds as though you are dismissing his compliment and b) he might think, Oh yeah, I hadn't noticed before, but you are short/fat/ugly!

✔ Keep your conversations light and fun.

Don't:

✘ Take a friend along.

✘ Ask questions that are too personal in the beginning— like: Are you still a virgin? And don't make personal comments about his appearance unless it's complimentary—asking if he's always had sticky out ears isn't going to make him feel great, whereas asking where he gets his hair cut as it looks fab, is.

✘ Steal his thunder if he's telling you a joke, by saying, "Oh, I've heard this," or finishing the punch-line for him. Let him get it out and laugh. It's his first date too and he's probably a bit nervous.

✖ Make him feel bad if he says something dumb as sometimes the wrong thing slips out and you don't want to make him feel totally stupid.

✖ Be too early and don't be too late.

The Art of Good Conversation

A girl came home from a party complaining about one
of the guests. "She must have yawned about fifty
times while I was talking to her."
"Maybe she wasn't yawning," suggested her
mate. "Maybe she was trying to say something."

As with the flirting, once again, don't
talk about yourself non-stop. It's easy to do this because of
nerves or to fill awkward silences. A good conversation is a two-
way street. You listen. You talk. You ask questions. Keep it light—
mutual interests, fave music, movies, etc. Get to know each
other. However, there is also a saying that goes: a gossip talks
about others, a bore talks about himself and a good conversationalist talks (or asks) about you. So, in the early part of the
date there's no harm in getting him talking about himself as
much as you can, as it will make him feel like: a) he's really
interesting, and b) you're really interested. As the dates continue,
though, make sure that the communication is going both ways
or else you will end up getting bored or resentful. Also don't
gossip in a mean way about people you know or else he might

think, If she's saying things like that about them, what's she going to say about me?

If you're really shy and are truly lost for words when you are with someone you fancy, don't worry, you can always bluff it.

Over to my brother, Tony, for this bit, as he's the world's best bluffer!

The Insider's Guide to Good Conversation

by Tony Williams

1. Feed leading questions to your date and listen to their replies. Feed him lines that get him going on his fave subject. For example, for a boy who is movie mad: "What are your top three favorite films?" You get the idea. If you do it right, he won't even notice that you're shy or don't have a lot to say. For example . . .

   Right:

   He: Are you into movies?

   You: Oh yes. What are your favorite three?

   He: (Ten-minute animated reply.)

You: Mmm. Fascinating. And what's the worse movie you've ever seen?

He: (Five-minute animated reply.)

You: Wow. You really know a lot about films.

He: (Thinks: What an impressive and easy to talk to girl.)

Wrong:

He: Are you into movies?

You: Nah. Not really.

(End of conversation.)

Also wrong:

He: Are you into movies?

You: Sometimes, but I prefer the telly. My favorites are . . . (Ten minutes of you blabbering on.)

He: Oh, I don't watch those.

You: Oh, let me fill you in on what you've been missing. (More blabbering on.)

He: (Thinks: We haven't got a lot in common here.)

Remember, a good listener waits for their turn to speak, keeps eye contact ,doesn't interrupt and doesn't look bored or look round the room.

2. If he asks you leading questions about his favorite interest, don't be afraid to say that you don't know about a subject or else you can end up looking like a prat. Once again, ask him to tell you about it.

(**NB:** We girls think this is good only in the initial stages of pulling if you are feeling a bit nervous. After that it has to be two-way with talking and listening on both sides. And remember if out with a group of mates, be careful not to exclude your date if he doesn't know the people you might be talking about. You could be having a jolly old time and a great laugh, but there's nothing worse than feeling that you can't join in the conversation.)

So, he's asked you out, you're prepared to talk, listen and look fab. What's the best place for a first date? Tony reckons he's done a lot of research into this.

Tony's Top Romantic Places

I reckon that it's best to go some place where you can get to know each other so, although a movie might seem like a good idea, you're not going to get much chance to talk. On the other hand, if it's a horror film you do get to snuggle up and if your date doesn't have much to say, it removes the embarrassment of long silences—and at least you have the movie to talk about when you come out.

Here are my fave places for a first date:

- Anywhere candlelit.
- A meal in a cosy little restaurant with a relaxed atmosphere.
- The local park on a summer's night. (You can snog behind the trees.)
- A funky old café with big sofas you can sink into.

- Bowling can be good fun as you get to talk and play (but not in Lucy's case as when she lets the ball go it goes up instead of across and once, she almost knocked out a guy in the next lane).

- My bedroom—I have some great sounds and it's very private.

(**Note from Nesta:** Obviously, this last one works only for Tony as he has got it kitted out like a cool bachelor pad. If your bedroom is a tip, think twice.

Also it might give a boy ideas about what your intentions are!)

Snogging

And so to kissing. We thought we'd hand this bit over to Tony too, seeing as he thinks he's such an expert. (Lucy says he is!)

How to be a Great Kisser
by Tony Williams

okay, girls, this is how it's done!

Do:

- ✔ Have clean teeth and fresh breath.
- ✔ Vary the intensity of your kisses (gentle to more searching and deeper, back to gentle again). There's nothing worse than someone who just goes for it with the same pressure all the time.
- ✔ Close your eyes. (There's nothing weirder than someone eyeballing you mid-snog.)
- ✔ Leave him wanting more.

Don't:

✗ Give gooey, sloppy kisses with your mouth open too wide. Yuck.

✗ Kiss when you've been eating garlic, curry, onions or tuna or been smoking. Yuck. (If you can't avoid one of them, like if you've been to an Indian restaurant, chew some gum.)

✗ Pin him down so he can't breathe.

✗ Kiss with your mouth tight shut.

✗ Outstay your welcome.

Your First Kiss

This is a good chance to test if the chemistry really is there.

• Relax. Sometimes it's nice if he puts his arms around your waist and you put yours around his neck.

• Start with a soft, closed mouth, then let it open a little (not a lot).

• A first kiss should last more than a second so that it's not a peck, and less than ten seconds. If it's too short, you may be giving the message that he's not for you. If it's too long at this stage, he may think that you're over keen.

• After this kiss, you can decide if you want more.

+2 × Second Kiss

Start as before—remember to keep your lips soft, not too puckered up and keep your arms around each other. This time your kisses can last longer, but remember to keep breathing or come up for breath in between a row of kisses. You don't have to go for a snogathon at this stage as it's nice to break between kisses and just hold each other or hold hands and savour the moment.

French Kissing

- Take into consideration points mentioned before: fresh breath, relax, etc. Let go of tension in your neck or head.

  1er étage

- Put your arms around each other.

  2ieme étage

- Start off with a normal, soft kiss with a closed mouth, then part your lips a little.

  3ieme étage

- If the boys has his lips closed, you can nudge his lips apart gently with your tongue. But don't force it.

- Move your tongue inside the boy's mouth and gently touch his tongue. Don't use the tongue as a

  tour eiffel étage

61

poker. You don't have to clean his teeth with your tongue or stick your tongue down his throat!

- If he seems tense or moves away, stop. If he seems to like it, continue.

- You can open your mouth a little wider if you feel that the boy is responding and keep on doing what you're doing with a little more passion. Take your lead from each other, i.e. whether to go slower or deeper with your kisses. You don't need to open your mouth very wide as this isn't a resuscitation exercise, it is a kiss.

- Don't forget to swallow and come up for air when you need.

- Go with the flow. You may want to close your mouth again and just go back to soft kisses, then back to French kissing—whatever feels natural.

- And even though Izzie felt embarrassed about the fact she practised kissing on the back of her hand, it's actually not a bad idea! You can experience what feels good and what feels strange.

- If you have braces, you can still French kiss. You just have to be a bit more careful and not as forceful. If he wears braces too, avoid touching the teeth.

And that's it. Simple, really.

Cosmic Kisses
by Izzie Foster

I'm sending you cosmic kisses straight from my heart
A planet collision won't tear us apart
The distance between us is never too far
I'll hitch a ride on a comet to get where you are

In a moment a glance became a kiss
In a heartbeat I knew my world had changed
For better, forever there is no other
You're one in a million, of that I'm sure
One a million and I'm feeling so secure

Cos I'm sending you cosmic kisses straight from my heart
A planet collision won't tear us apart
The distance between us is never too far
I'll hitch a ride on a comet to get where you are

How to Get a Second Date

- Put into practice everything we've said so far for your first date, i.e. be lighthearted, fun and interesting; look your best; don't overstay your welcome; leave him wanting more. If he has to go home at a certain time, don't complain—in fact, it's best if you leave first.

- Be cool. Don't assume that because you've had one date that you are now "in a relationship" and have licence to call him three times a day and see him four times a week. Give him lots of space in the beginning because one thing that most boys don't like is feeling pressurised to be committed before they're ready. You might be over the moon and in love, and think he's The One but bide your time.

- When a mate says I'll call you, she often means when I get home or tomorrow, but it's different with dates. If your first date went well, he'll call you, but remember when a boy says he'll call you he means probably in a week, earlier if he's really keen, so don't panic.

- Alternatively, if he says he'd like to see you again after your first date, say casually, okay, sure, I'll give you a call and you take his number. Then wait a while, at least a few days. Let him sweat about why his phone isn't ringing!

How to Keep Him

And so it's love. The real thing. You're dating. You've become a couple. You say things like, "Love makes the world go round." Round the bend, your friends might think, so make sure you don't shove them out as you go into a couple bubble. As you spend more time together and get to know each other better, it can be quite a readjustment having a "steady boyfriend" to fit into the rest of your life. We asked Lucy's mum to do this bit as she works as a counselor and spends her days giving couples good advice about how to make relationships work!

Mrs. Lovering's Top Tips for Relationships

- Remember that relationships are a two-way street, so don't always demand your own way about where you go and who you hang out with. And don't always let him have his own way or hang out with his friends. Find what suits both of you.

- Negotiate: if you want to see him four nights a week and he wants to see you one, work out an arrangement that suits both of you.

- Keep communicating: if something's bothering you, don't bottle it up, talk about it. Don't grumble, there's nothing like it for killing romance. If you have something to say, say it clearly and without blame. Sentences that start with "I feel . . ." or "I need . . ." work much better than accusative words like "You *should* have . . ." or "*You* ought . . ." as they can put a boy on the defensive.

- Don't bury yourself away with your boyfriend. See your friends regularly. Remember, boys may come and go, but friends are forever and there when you need them to pick up the pieces if things go wrong.

- Don't expect your boyfriend to keep you happy on *every* level, then blame him if he can't. We all have different facets to our personalities and some you can share with a new boy, some you will share with your mates.

- If you're feeling down or angry, find ways to let off steam without blasting it all out on your boyfriend. Just because you are dating, doesn't mean you can dump on him or vice versa.

- Give each other regular acknowledgement for what each of you contributes. Don't only say what's missing or what hasn't been done.

- Respect your boyfriend as an individual and don't try to change him. The only time you can change a boy is when he's a baby.

- Make time to talk. And listen.

- Treat each other to occasional surprises.

- Make an effort sometimes to go out of your way to let your boyfriend know you think he's special. If his favorite ice cream is Ben & Jerry's Peanut Butter Cup, get him a tub.

- Don't always expect him to pay because he's male.

- Don't be clingy. There's a saying that goes, "If you love someone, let them go. If they come back, it's meant to be. If they don't, it isn't". In plain language, that means give him space.

- Maintain some independence and keep up your interests outside the relationship.

- Don't criticize him in front of his or your mates. It might feel safe to say something negative if there's a crowd there, but it can be very humiliating for the one being criticized.

- Don't be controlling and don't be controlled about what you wear, who you see or what you want to do. You're both individuals and neither of you own each other just because you're dating.

And a Few More Words From Tony . . .

Some girls can get over-sensitive when a boy is short on the phone and then think he's gone off her. Sometimes it's simply that she's called at a bad time. Pick a good time for your calls:

- Don't call too early in the morning when your boyfriend and his family are in a rush to get out.

- Don't call too late or else you may get his parents, then he has to explain all about you and may feel embarrassed about being grilled.

- Don't call when there's an important football match or his favorite TV program is on.
- Don't call when you know he's with a bunch of mates as sometimes boys act clever and cool on the phone. Don't ask me why—us boys can be stupid like that.

Sex

It's a big decision whether you want to take the relationship further and when you want to have sex—although sixteen is the legal age of consent in the UK (seventeen in Northern Ireland). All of us girls have had to deal with boys and their wandering hands before we're ready. We think that you should have sex only when you really and truly feel ready and you want to do it. In the meantime, there are many ways you can be close without actually having sex. Try massaging, cuddling, stroking each other and discover how to be sensual with each other without having to go the whole way.

- Don't be pressurised to have sex for fear that he will drop you. If that's the only reason he's with you, he's not worth it.
- Don't feel pressured to have sex because you're the last virgin on the planet (or feel like you are). Different people are ready at different times and not everyone who says they've done it, actually has.
- Don't give way to emotional blackmail if he says things like you're too young, immature, innocent to have sex or that you won't go with him because you're frigid or a lesbian.
- And if you do decide to go ahead, here's a quick word from TJ's mum, Dr. Watts.

Note From Dr. Watts

I see a lot of teens in my surgery and can appreciate that one of the biggest decisions that you girls have to make is whether and when to have sex. By the time I see girls, more often than not, they've already made that decision and either want to talk about birth control or have left it too late, got pregnant or caught some type of STI (sexually transmitted infection). It's amazing that in this "enlightened age," when people are supposed to know about contraception, a high percentage of women still get pregnant unintentionally.

Almost all of them say, "Well, I didn't think it would happen to me," and some say, "I didn't think I could get pregnant the first time." Think again. If you decide to have sex and you don't want to have a baby or catch an STI, then you *must* use protection. Some methods of contraception are ninety-nine percent effective at preventing pregnancy, but effectiveness varies depending on which method you use. None of the methods are totally guaranteed, and only one protects against STIs (condoms). In fact, the only one hundred-percent effective method is abstinence, i.e. no sexual contact, as then there is no opportunity for sperm to fertilise an egg, and no means of passing on infection.

Remember, only you can make the decision as to whether or not you really want to have sex. It may seem like everyone's doing it—at school, on the TV, at parties—and you may feel like you have to do it as well just to feel accepted. However, don't let pressure from friends, either boys or girls, push you into it before you feel the time is right. You can still have a relationship with someone without having to have sex. The decision is a personal choice and if someone cares about you, they will respect whatever choice you make.

If you do decide to go ahead, it is essential to use protection.

essential!

You can get all the information on the methods of contraception available—free of charge and anonymously—by dropping into your local Family Planning Clinic and picking up a leaflet.

A small girl went to her mother to ask why her stomach was so swollen.

"It's because Daddy has given me a baby," she explained.

The little girl looked distressed and went running to her father in the next room. "Daddy, you know that baby you gave Mummy?"

"Yes, dear," he says.

"She's eaten it," the girl cries.

When Relationships Go Wrong
Tell-tale Signs a Relationship Is Over

- He stops calling you.
- He stops turning up to see you!
- It feels flat when you kiss.

- You always argue about petty things.
- You decide you don't want to be in a committed relationship and the relationship is getting too serious for you.

corrosive

- Your boyfriend treats you thoughtlessly, is always late, puts you down in front of his friends, or pressures you to go further than you want to.
- You have little to say to each other any more.
- You've met someone else.
- He's met someone else (or several someone elses).

Cut the Connection

by Izzie Foster

You think you're going out tonight, but you'll be staying in
You'll sigh, you'll cry, you'll wonder why the phone will never ring.

You know he's playing games like every other boy,
But you don't care, though you're aware he treats you like a toy

He says he'll be there for you when all the chips are down
But he's said the same to every girl in town

He doesn't care you're in despair as tears burn in your eyes
You'll sigh, you'll cry you'll wonder why all he says is lies

Cut the connection, turn off the phone, grab hold of life and you won't be alone
Believe in yourself and no one else and you'll find that you have grown.
So cut the connection, turn off phone, grab hold of life and you won't be alone

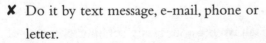

How to Tell Him It's Over

If you do want to end your relationship, the best way to tell him is in person as soon as possible as it's not fair to keep someone hanging on or not knowing where they stand. It's never easy telling someone it's over, but the sooner it's dealt with, the better.

Do:

✔ Be clear and direct about it. Saying vague things like, "Oh, I can't make it this week, I'm busy," simply means to him that you're not free this week, but probably will be next week.

✔ Give him a reason—any of the above from the tell tale signs it's over: e.g. We always argue, We have nothing to say to each other, I'm not ready for a serious relationship, etc.

Don't:

✘ Do it by text message, e-mail, phone or letter.

✘ Get a friend to do it for you.

✘ Just stand him up—you'd hate it if that happened to you.

And Lal insisted that we included these lines that he found on the Internet to say goodbye as he thought they were hilariously funny. All we can say is that these are lines that you should definitely *not* to use to break up with someone.

- Kind, intelligent, loving and hot—this describes everything you're not.
- I love your smile, your face, and your eyes—wahey, I'm good at telling lies!
- I see your face when I am dreaming—that's why I always wake up screaming.

Yeah, right, Lal. You have mucho to learn.

Dealing With Rejection

Rejection can really hurt and it's hard not to take it personally. Here's how we think it's best to deal with it.

Lucy: Allow yourself twenty-four hours' sobbing, gnashing of teeth, wailing, listening to sad songs, eating ice cream, watching sloppy tragic films. Kick a few cushions. Feel *very* sorry for yourself. As soon as your twenty-four hours are up, then you stop. Let go. Move on. Life is too short to be miserable over some boy who hasn't got the good taste to want you. Plus there are others out there— plenty more fish in the sea.

Izzie: Eat chocolate. Plenty of it. Spend time with your mates, having a laugh about it all. And give it time. Time mends a broken heart.

Nesta: Think that it's his loss and go out and pull someone else to distract you.

TJ: Be philosophical. If it wasn't meant to be, it wasn't meant to be. You can't make someone fancy you or want to go out with you. It can hurt like hell and you can wonder what's wrong with you, but nothing *is* wrong with you. He just wasn't the right boy at this time. Someone else will come along sooner or later.

Damaged Beauty

by Izzie Foster

He's frequently flawless, but often unkind
This fallen angel drives you out of your mind
He's the devil beneath you and you ought to know
He has to go, you really should know

The gift you are given is kindness and grace
But each time you fall for a handsome young face
Stop looking for light in love's gloomy rooms
Throw open the windows
Let in the sun, you're number one

Look into your heart, just make a start,
You really know, he has to go
Put your damaged beauty in a silent place

There's new love just waiting get back in the race
Shout out you're ready, cast into the pool
This time remember, don't land a fool
Look into your heart, make a brand new start,
Look into your heart, it's up to you.

Revenge

We just had to put this section in for a bit of devilry, though of course, as responsible and mature teenagers, we would never actually dream of doing any of the following. (Heh, heh!)

Nesta: Put fresh prawns into his duvet. He'll go mad trying to find out where the smell is coming from after a few days.

TJ: Sew up the ankles of his trousers.

Lucy: Tie his shoelaces together.

Izzie: I don't think revenge is good for the soul. Forgiveness is better. But then if I were *pushed* to carry out a revenge, I reckon you can't beat getting hold of his mobile, then phoning the speaking clock in Hong Kong.

And so there is all that we've learnt about pulling boys and what to do with them once you've got them. However, if you still feel like you need a bit more help, it's over to Mystic Iz.

Boys and Astrology
by Izzie Foster

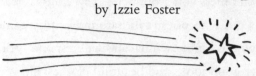

okay. So this is what I think. Learning a boy's star sign can sometimes give you some insight in to what he's about and ensure that as far as he's concerned, you're ahead of the game.

Aries (21 March–20 April):

Aries is the sign of the ram and they are known for leaping before they look so you probably won't have to wait around too long if this boy is interested. However, sometimes he can enjoy the chase more than the conquest and will move on because he gets easily bored. He certainly wouldn't like a girl who's too dependent or clingy. His key word is *energy* and his ideal girl would be confident—someone who can stand up to him and be his equal.

Taurus (21 April–21 May): Taurus is the sign of the bull and you won't find a more loyal (or stubborn) boy. A Taurean

boy can be very slow to make up his mind, but when he does, he won't mess you around. His key word is *stability* and he'll want a girl who doesn't flirt around or play games. He's also a boy who is highly sensual and will respond well to fabulous scents, good looks and beautiful clothes. However, you might need to push him into trying new things and getting out and about as he can be set in his ways and sticks with what he knows.

Gemini **(22 May–21 June):** Gemini is the sign of the twins and a Gemini boy will be lively, quick-witted and entertaining. He's turned on more by the mental than the physical. His key word is *flirtatious* and his is a sign that is likely to have many admirers. He likes change and variety so is not the easiest boy to get to commit. His ideal girl is someone bright who can floor him with witty one-liners, who is a good communicator who will keep him well entertained

Cancer **(22 June–22 July):** Cancer is the sign of a crab and like the crab, can hide behind a tough 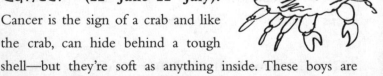 shell—but they're soft as anything inside. These boys are home-loving, their key word is *security* and they will respond well to lots of affection and hugs. His ideal will be a supportive girl who will cherish him and give him space for his occasional crabby moods.

Leo **(23 July–23 August):** Leo is the sign of the lion. This is a boy who likes to be at the centre of attention. He has high expectations of love and can feel very  sorry for himself if let down in any way—like a lion with a sore paw. His key word is *ego* and when he falls in love it can be full on. His ideal girl is a real glam puss who will adore him and improve his self- image with her charisma.

Virgo **(24 August–23 September):** Virgo is the sign of the virgin and a Virgo boy can be very choosy (and critical) before he commits himself. His key word is *perfection* and he may happily analyse and talk about relationships, unlike some of the other signs. His ideal girl would be intelligent, emotionally calm and tidy in her habits.

Libra **(24 September–23 October):** Libra is the sign of the scales. These boys are flirts and can charm the birds out of the trees, but they can also be indecisive and end up causing chaos by not making up their minds about what or who they want. His key word is *beauty* and he has great expectations for love. If he thinks he's found it, he will give it in abundance and will expect the same back. If thwarted, he can be cool and impersonal. He forms relationships swiftly, but can just as easily abandon them. His ideal girl is a romantic soul with great style who is prepared to give as much as she gets.

Scorpio (24 October–22 November):

Scorpio is the sign of the scorpion. This boy can be a mystery and at times it may be hard to read him. However, when he falls in love, it is deeply, loyally (and possessively). He's a boy who will do anything for the right girl and isn't someone who will let go easily if he feels you're the one for him. His key word is *magnetism* and his ideal girl is someone who can intrigue him and can handle all-encompassing passion (and some jealousy).

Sagittarius (23 November–21 December): Sagittarius

is the sign of the archer. This is a boy who loves spontaneity and adventures and when it comes to falling in love,

Sagittarians can be up and down like a yo-yo. He's not one to hold back and can be loving and generous, but can sometimes come across as blunt or clumsy. His key word is *freedom* and he'll be looking for a girl who will share his love of excitement. He's not one to be caged in or tied down.

Capricorn (22 December–20 January): Capricorn is

the sign of the goat. This boy can be ambitious and hard working. When it comes to love, he can be slow to show his feelings through fear of rejection, but once hooked will be loyal and caring. His key word is *conscientious*. He'll be looking for a responsible girl who doesn't mess him about and who has her own status and goals whilst admiring him for his.

Aquarius (21 January–19 February): Aquarius is the

sign of the waterbearer. This boy has an endlessly curious mind and will be into discovering what he can about the world (the more unusual the better). His key word is *friendship*, but in love can sometimes appear to be distant and uninterested—any displays of excess emotion will frighten him right off. His ideal is a girl who will fascinate him with her knowledge and experience. He wants a cool companion to go off making discoveries with.

Pisces **(20 February–20 March):** Pisces is the sign of the fish. This boy can be romantic and poetic, but can fall in and out of love quickly as he searches for his perfect girl. His key word is *mystical*. He may have high expectations about fairy tale love and his ideal is a sensitive girl with dreamy eyes who shares his romantic fantasies.

Spells to Handle Boys

by Izzie Foster

And if you still feel like you need help, there's always some hocus-pocus to try.

Spell One: To Attract a Boy

1. Write his name seven times on a piece of paper.
2. Put the paper in an envelope or even better, in a locket, if you have one.
3. Carry the envelope (or wear the locket) for seven days and nights after which time, he should come to you.

Spell Two: To Make Someone Love You

1. Get a candle and a bottle of oil (almond or olive).
2. Pour a little oil into your hand and rub it into the unlit candle with your hands whilst think-ing thoughts of love about the boy you like.

3. Carve into the side of the candle your wish. e.g. I want John Smith to fancy me.
4. Light the candle and by the time it's burnt down, your wish will come true.

Spell Three: For Boys Who Need Warming Up a Bit

1. Write his name and yours in a heart on a piece of paper.
2. Put the paper in a warm place for seven days, e.g. where your boiler is kept or on top of a radiator.

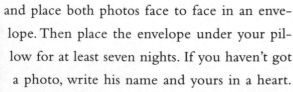

3. By the end of the week, he will be feeling extremely warm towards you.

Spell Four: For Boys Who Need to Sweeten up Towards You

1. This time you ideally need photographs. One of you and one of him. Sprinkle his photo with sugar (any kind) and place both photos face to face in an envelope. Then place the envelope under your pillow for at least seven nights. If you haven't got a photo, write his name and yours in a heart.

Put in an envelope with the sugar, then as before, place it under your pillow.

2. By the end of the week, the boy will be sweet on you.

Spell Five: For Over-Amorous Boys Who Need to Cool Down

1. Get either a lock of his hair and a lock of yours or a photo of him and a photo of you.

2. Put both in an envelope or freezer bag.

3. Put in the freezer for seven days.

4. By the end of the week, his feelings for you will have cooled off.

Note from Lucy: I tried Spell Five once when I wanted Tony to cool down and I swear he cooled down so much he went off me. I then tried the sweetening up spell and although he did come round again, my bed was covered in bits of sugar for weeks after. When I told Mum about it, she wasn't very pleased and said I'd attract mice. I told her I'd attracted a rat (as I wasn't very happy with Tony at that time), but Mum wasn't amused!

Note from Tony: I always knew girls were witches.

Note from Steve: When using a computer, do witches run spell check?

Note from Izzie: If you guys don't watch out, I'll turn you into frogs.

Staying Together
by Izzie Foster

Hey there, don't you know, that boys just come and boys just go
But friends stay together forever and ever
Hey there, follow the noise and you'll soon find a gang of boys.

Had enough of football chants?
Smelly trainers, mindless rants?
Boys are stupid, boys are vain
A dozen boys share just one brain
No boys!

Yes, girlfriend—it's the truth, we're not going to waste our youth
Friends stay together forever and ever
We're too pretty, we're too smart
to let any boyfriend break us apart

Boys are stupid boys are vain
A dozen boys just share one brain
No boys!

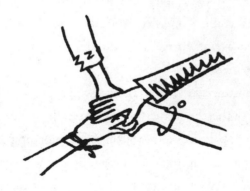

Mates
by all of us!

And so to the most important relationships in our lives. Mates.

The best bit of advice we've ever heard about friendship is: if you want a friend, be a friend.

It works if you already have friends and it works if you want to find some. Basically, it means: be the kind of friend you always hoped you'd have and you'll soon find that you have loads and you get on great. Another way of putting it is, do unto others as you'd have them do unto you. Amen. Or as Nest says: Ah, men.

If you want to make new friends, it won't hurt to put into practice a lot of the tips in the first section of this guide, about meeting boys (apart from the flirting and snogging). Once again, you're not going to meet anyone if you stay at home wondering why you haven't got any mates. Get out there. Walk your dog in the park. Join clubs. Join dance classes or whatever you're into. Talk to people. Accept invites to parties—in fact, throw your own party. Make things happen. Make an effort.

Once you have your mates, then don't expect them to do all the work. Friendship, like all relationships, is a two-way street.

- Don't expect your mate always to call you. Call her often.

- Don't be a fair-weather friend, i.e. only there for a laugh and good times. Be aware of when she's feeling low and be supportive.

- Don't expect your mate to always plan everything. Plan things together.

- Don't go out with a mate's ex unless she is okay with it and gives her approval.

- Never try and get off with a mate's boyfriend.

- Keep talking, no matter what. Sometimes you might think that you're all alone in what you're going through, but a problem shared is a problem halved. Mates are there for each other.

- Don't shove your mate or plans you've made with your mate aside the minute a cute boy comes along. She will feel like she's way down on the list of your priorities and doesn't matter. Remember—your mates are the ones who are there for you if things don't work out and it's not fair to expect that if she's been pushed aside while you "had better things to do."

- Ask for help when you need it. No one's psychic. (Except Izzie. Maybe.)

Ground Rules
for Being Out with Mates

- Be aware of each other. Don't abandon a mate if a group of you have gone out together and three of you get off with boys and the fourth doesn't. You can always arrange to see the boys another time or spend time with the boys as a group so you aren't leaving your mate sitting there like a lemon on her own.

- Get your round in. Don't let one mate always pay for drinks or snacks. Be aware of when it's your turn, unless something has been agreed beforehand because one of you is Miss Loadsamoney and doesn't mind paying.

- Keep an eye on each other's drinks and don't accept drinks from strangers as sometimes they can be spiked.

- Agree on secret hand signals before you go out to indicate to each other if you need rescuing because you are bored out of your mind or some boy is coming on too strong. It's also useful to have a signal for when you like someone and want to be left alone with him for a while. If you are out with boys who are friends as opposed to boyfriends, you can ask them if they will help if a boy is coming on too strong, by pretending that they are with you on a date.

- If one mate gets off with a boy the rest of you don't know, keep an eye out for where she is.
- Always make sure that all your mates have got a lift home or are travelling home together.
- Keep talking to each other, even one of you has gone weird or is feeling blue.

And there it is. Relationships sorted!

Part Two
Beauty, Health, and Fashion

by Izzie Foster
and Lucy Lovering

Beauty

For this section, it's over to Izzie and me (Lucy). I want to work in the fashion industry when I leave school and I already make my own clothes so fashion is my thing! And to Izzie—because natural remedies are her thing. She has picked my dad's brain (yuck!) as he runs the local health food shop and with his help, she has come up with loads of natural (and inexpensive) ways of looking after yourself.

We all try to schedule in one day or evening a month to go through a beautifying routine. We usually do it on a Sunday or when it's raining or there's not a lot to do and it can be great fun (especially seeing the girls covered in some of my home-made avocado or banana gloops dripping from their faces).

So here goes: how to be blindingly beautiful *à la* Lucy and Izzie (and Lucy's dad).

Looking After Your Skin

by Izzie

(All the items mentioned in this section should be easily available at your local health food shop!)

You don't need loads of dosh to have fabulous skin. A good routine of cleansing and moisturising at night as well as a healthy diet will keep it looking good. Some people believe what you eat can affect your skin and a break-out of spots often can be related to eating too much sugar, greasy or junk food.

Top Tips for Brilliant Skin

- Eat lots of fresh fruit and vegetables as they are rich in vitamins and minerals. Broccoli and spinach might not be your thing, but they will make your skin look much better than a diet of pizza, crisps, and takeaways will. (Sad, but true.)

- Drink at least a litre of water a day. Your eyes will sparkle and your skin will glow.

- Fresh juice: if you have a juicer, you can make your own fresh juice and it will really perk up your complexion. My favorite is fresh grape, Lucy's is carrot and apple, TJ's is carrot, celery, apple and ginger and Nesta's is orange. They really do taste fantastic.

Eat/Drink in Moderation:

- Sweets
- Chocolate
- Crisps
- Junk food
- Fizzy drinks
- Fried foods

Do:

✔ Get regular exercise
✔ Get enough sleep
✔ Drink plenty of water

Avoid:

✘ Over-exposure to the sun without protection.
✘ Smoking. (If you want good skin, don't smoke. There is nothing more aging, not to mention lethal for your health. I once saw photographs of twins in their forties. The one who hadn't smoked looked about ten years younger than the one who had.)

> Her face looked like a million dollars.
> (All green and wrinkled.)

Routines for Different Skin Types

Lucy's dad recommends using essential oils. These are aromatic substances which have been extracted from various plant sources such as fruits and herbs, tree bark and roots and are available at most health food stores and some chemist's. They are also known as aromatherapy oils and all of them have beneficial healing properties. Essential oils are potent and if used undiluted can sting, so it recommended that for use on the skin, they are diluted in what's called a base oil, which is an unscented oil (such as grape seed, olive, sunflower and apricot, almond or peach kernel).

The price of essential oils can vary a lot—for example, a bottle of rosemary or lavender is quite inexpensive, whereas rose or frankincense is more expensive. This is because some of the herbs or flowers used in the making of the oils are more readily available than others. When you first see bottles of essential oils in shops, you may think, Whoa!, they're costly for such tiny bottles, but they do last for ages, as you only need a couple of drops at a time. My favorites (rose, jasmine, neroli) are slightly more

101

expensive, but it takes sacks and sacks and *sacks* of the flower petals to make the oil into such a pure concentrated form and since they are so strong, you need only a tiny bit in your base oil. My rose oil, for example, has lasted me nearly a whole year.

Finding Your Skin Type

An easy way to find out what type of skin you have is to wipe your face with a tissue first thing in the morning. If there is oil on it, you have greasy skin, if there is no grease on the tissue, you have normal or dry skin. If you're not sure if your skin is dry or normal, wash it with an ordinary soap (i.e.: not a special moisturising type or a kind for oily skin) and water. If it feels slightly parched and tight afterwards, your skin is dry. If it feels smooth and supple, your skin is normal.

Dry Skin

The cause: Dry skin comes about because the sebaceous glands are underactive and unable to produce the oil needed to prevent the skin losing moisture.

The solution: Essential oils and moisturizers will encourage the glands to function normally again, as well as moisturising and nourishing the skin. As well as cleansing and moisturising, a course of cod liver oil tablets or Vitamin E tablets can be effective.

Avoid: Sun, sunbeds, overheated houses, smoking.

Cleansing: This is best done with a mild cream skin cleanser or an oatmeal or almond soap.

Toner: Camomile, rosewater or rosehip toner.

Moisturizing: Feeding the skin is essential for your skin type so apply moisturizer in the morning and at night, nourish the skin with a rich cream for dry skin. If you put it on when you get into your bath, the steam will help the cream absorb into the skin.

Essential oils for Dry Skin: Geranium, rose, sandalwood, neroli, patchouli, ylang-ylang, camomile. (Add four to six drops of any of these to your usual moisturizer, a base oil or an unscented moisturizer from the health store.)

Base Oils: If you want to really treat your skin, you can make up your own oil to apply in the evening. (As with the moisturizer, you can add any of the essential oils mentioned above to a base oil below.)

- Jojoba—leaves a lovely satiny feeling.
- Avocado—is rich and nourishing.
- Sweet almond—is easily absorbed.
- Hazelnut—is rich in Vitamin E which is good for dry skin.

Also, if you add wheatgerm oil to your base oil, it will help preserve it (ten percent wheatgerm to ninety percent base oil).

Weekly mask: Use a nourishing or moisturising mask from the chemist's or make up your own from a cup of oatmeal, a tablespoon of almond oil, water and four drops of the essential oils for dry skin. Mix and apply to the face and leave for ten minutes. Remove with warm water.

Greasy Skin

The cause: In the case of oily skin, the sebaceous glands are overactive and produce excess oil.

The solution: Essential oils will help redress the imbalance and aid the glands in working normally. It is important to keep the skin clean so that the pores don't get clogged with dust, makeup or debris. The antiseptic properties in essential oils helps keep infection in check, help to prevent spots and pimples.

Don't overdo the cleansing, though. Many people with greasy skin try to get their skin as dry as possible and remove all traces of oiliness. This starts a vicious circle as the sebaceous glands will only try to produce more oil to replace what is being lost or removed. The solution is to rebalance the glands with the right essential oils and try and keep the skin bacteria free.

Avoid: Coffee, sugar, chocolate, spicy food and fatty foods. For some people, cutting out cheese helps tremendously.

Cleansing: Be meticulous about keeping your skin clean. In the morning, wash with soap and water and in the evening, clean with a cleanser.

Toner: Orange water or witch hazel.

Moisturising: Often, isn't necessary for people with greasy skin to use moisturizer as the skin is producing enough oil on its own. If you have dry areas on your skin and do want to use a moisturizer, use one with the word "noncomedogenic" or "nonacnegenic" on the label as these products help prevent spots.

Essential Oils for Greasy Skin: Lemon, bergamot, juniper, geranium, lavender, sandalwood, tea tree. (Lavender is particularly good for healing if there is any scarring from spots on the face.) Add four to six drops of one, or a combination to your usual moisturizer.

Base Oils: People with oily skin prefer the lighter oils that are more easily absorbed. Add four drops of the essential oil mentioned above to a tablespoon of base oil.

- Grapeseed—very light
- Apricot or peach kernel—as both are easily absorbed.

Steaming the skin is a good way to keep pores clear. Add a few drops of juniper, lemon or lavender oil to a bowl of boiling water, cover your head with a towel and immerse your face in the steam, coming up for air when you need or if it feels too hot. Splash the skin with cold water afterwards to close the pores.

A hot compress can also be used. Take a clean flannel which has been soaked in hot water to which a few drops of your essential oil has been added. Place the hot flannel over your face for a few minutes. Again, afterwards, splash the skin with cold water to close the pores.

Normal Skin

The Cause: Everything is working well—a good diet, good health and good care—though very few people have a completely perfect skin. It usually tends to be on the dry side or greasy. It is still important to look after the skin, though, whatever the condition.

Routine: Regular cleansing, toning, moisturising and use of essential oils.

Cleansing: You can use plain soap and water in the morning and use a cleansing cream or lotion for normal skin in the evening.

Toner: Rosewater or orange water.

Moisturising: Any moisturizer for normal skin could be used in the morning and evening.

Essential Oils for Normal Skin: Rose, lavender, lemon, neroli, rosewood, patchouli, ylang-ylang, petitgrain, bergamot. (Add a few drops of one or a combination of a few that you like to your moisturizer or a base oil for a boost to your skin.)

Base Oil: You can use whichever you like, although most people prefer the lighter ones such as peach or almond kernel or grapeseed. (Add four to six drops of essential oil to a tablespoon of base oil.)

If vegetable oil is made from vegetables, olive oil from olives, what is baby oil made from?

Baby oil

An Aromatic Facial Routine

Daily

1. Cleanse with your usual cleanser to which four to six drops of essential oils most suited to your skin type have been added. For example:

   Dry: Camomile and sandalwood.
   Greasy: Lavender and lemon.
   Normal: Rose and ylang-ylang.

2. Tone with a toner recommended for your skin type (you can also add a few drops of essential oil to your toner to make it extra effective). For example:

   Dry: Rosewater plus a few drops of camomile.
   Greasy: Witch hazel plus a few drops of juniper.
   Normal: Orange water plus a few drops of neroli.

3. Moisturize with a neutral base moisturizer to which you have added a few drops of essential oil that's suitable for your skin type. For example:

Dry: Moisturizer plus a few drops of geranium.

Greasy: Moisturizer plus a few drops of lemon.

Normal: Moisturizer plus a few drops of rose.

Weekly

1. Use a hot compress (a clean flannel soaked in hot water to which a few drops of the oils best for your skin type have been added). For example:

   Dry: Camomile.

   Greasy: Juniper.

   Normal: Rosewood.

2. Leave the flannel on the skin for five minute, then splash the skin with cold water to close the pores.

Monthly

1. Exfoliate to help remove dead cells from the surface of the skin. Either buy an exfoliating cream to which you can add the essential oils suitable for your skin type or you can make one. Here's how:

Homemade Exfoliator

- One cup of oatmeal (fine or coarse)
- One teaspoon of clear honey
- Half a cup of ground almonds

Mix the ingredients together. Add six drops of any oil that is good for your skin type. Apply to the face and gently massage in small circular movements. The coarseness of the almonds and oatmeal will gently remove the dead cells. After covering the whole face and neck, remove the exfoliator with warm water.

2. Use a face mask, particularly if you have dry skin. You can buy any moisturising mask from the local chemists or health food store or make one up from the examples below. Once again, you can add a few drops of the oil best for your skin type to your home made mask.

Firming Mask

- One egg yolk
- One tablespoon of Brewer's yeast
- One teaspoon of sunflower oil

Mix into a smooth paste. Apply to face and neck and leave for fifteen minutes, then rinse off.

NB: The yeast can stimulate the skin and draw out impurities, so it's not the best one to use before a big party in case it brings out any lurking spots.

Nourishing Mask

- One whole egg
- One teaspoon of honey
- One teaspoon of almond oil

Mix together, then apply. Leave on for fifteen minutes, then rinse off. (Can be a bit gloopy this one, so make sure you protect your clothing by putting a towel round your neck and shoulders in case it runs!)

Rejuvenating Mask

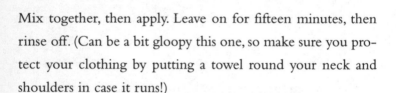

- Two tablespoons of ripe avocado flesh
- One teaspoon of honey
- Three drops of lemon juice

Mash the avocado and add the lemon juice, and the honey and mix into a paste. Apply and leave on for at least twenty minutes. (You may have to lie on the floor with a towel behind your head and neck for this one as it can be a bit runny.)

Banana Mask

(Especially good for dry skin)

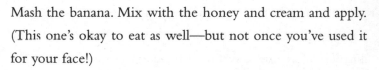

- Half a ripe banana
- One tablespoon of honey
- One tablespoon of double cream

Mash the banana. Mix with the honey and cream and apply. (This one's okay to eat as well—but not once you've used it for your face!)

For Bathtime

To keep your skin supple and soft all over, it's worth applying a body lotion regularly after your bath. You can use your essential oils in several ways at bathtime:

- Add six to eight drops to the water, swishing it round well.
- Add the drops to a base oil, which you can apply to your skin before you get in the bath. This helps the skin absorb the

oil, as the heat of the water will help the oils to penetrate.

- Add the essential oils to ready-made bases, e.g. bath oils or bubble baths and foams. It will make them even more aromatic if they are already scented.
- Add a few drops of essential oils to your body lotion and apply all over after your bath.

Getting the right scent is a bit like cooking. You have to experiment with your ingredients to get it right. Some of the oils are as stinky as disinfectant, but some of them smell sublime. These are our favorites for making bath time a really fragrant time: rose, jasmine, ylang-ylang, neroli, orange, bergamot, rosewood, geranium, sandalwood, patchouli.

Combining oils can also sometimes result in aromatic disasters, so here are some of tips for perfect combinations:

Refreshing: Rosemary and lemon or lime.

To aid sleep: Marjoram and lavender or camomile and lavender.

Relaxing: Lavender and rose.

Exotic: Ylang-ylang and patchouli.

Sensual: Ylang-ylang and sandalwood.

Soothing: Neroli and rosewood, or camomile and rose.

Uplifting: Jasmine and bergamot.

Balancing: Geranium and sandalwood.

Head-clearing: Peppermint and rosemary.

To combat sluggishness: Basil and juniper.

Problem Areas

Acne

Acne can be a real pain during teen years and beyond, but there are plenty of products now on the market to help deal with it.

Top Tips

- Wash your face twice a day with warm water and a soap especially made for acne. Pat dry. (Don't overwash as that can lead to irritation.)

- Don't try to cover acne up with heavy foundation as it can block the pores. If you feel you must for a special occasion, once again look for products with the words "noncomedogenic" or "nonacnegenic" on the label. (Generally, it's a good idea to look out for these words on any skin care or makeup produces you buy.)

- Don't pick your spots, no matter how tempting it is!

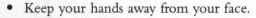

Popping pimples irritates the spot and can push bacteria further into the skin, leading to more swelling and redness and makes the whole thing last longer.

- Keep your hands away from your face.
- Keep your phone clean as it is an area where bacteria can build up.
- Keep glasses and sunglasses clean to prevent oil clogging pores around your nose and eyes.
- Keep all bed linen clean to get rid of oil build-up, dead skin, and dirt.
- Remove your makeup and cleanse every night so that your pores can breathe.
- Drink plenty of water.
- You can use cream that contains either benzoyl peroxide (destroys the bacteria that cause acne) or salicylic acid (helps to unclog pores and prevent spots).
- Keep your hair clean and out of your face.
- If your skin problem persists, it may be worth seeing a doctor or dermatologist as there are other options that they can recommend, and they'll help you find the best one for you.

Snog rash

(This is an irritation around the face and chin—usually arrives after a snog session with a boy who hasn't shaved!)

- Add two to three drops of rose or camomile oil (or both) to a bowl of warm water. Soak a face flannel in the water, then apply to the snog rash area for a few minutes. Both are very soothing oils so should help calm the area.

- Alternatively, add a few drops of the same oils to your moisturizer and apply to the area.

- Comfrey ointment or a calendula cream can both soothe an irritated skin. Both are available at most health food stores.

Bloodshot or Tired Eyes

- Soak two camomile tea bags in hot water. When the water has cooled, squeeze the tea bags out, lie back and place the bags over your closed eyes.

- Alternatively, cut two thin slices of cucumber. Lie back and place over closed eyes.

Blushing

Sadly, there aren't any cures for this. This is what us girls came up with on the subject:

Nesta: Wear pale makeup, although this can also make you look ill.

Lucy: Only go out in the dark (bit limiting, but it is an option).

Izzie: What you resist persists, so if you stop fighting it and even announce when it's going to happen—"I'm going to go red"—it will probably go away.

TJ: Um. Wear very bright red lipstick, that way when you blush, your face will match your lips. Okay. Not my best idea. I dunno. I think it's sweet when people blush.

To Tan or Not to Tan?

When the sun starts to shine, it is lovely to sit out and get a bit of color. However, all the experts advise that sun rays can be damaging so we thought that we'd ask Dr. Watts for her advice—so with this section, you can be prepared to enjoy the summer and stay safe.

Suntans

- Protection: It is important to protect your skin from the damaging rays of the sun. Overexposure can cause painful sunburn, can lead to premature wrinkling and increases the risk of developing skin cancer later in life. Just one bad sunburn in your youth can double the chances of developing skin cancer later, particularly if you are fair-skinned. A sunscreen of at least SPF 15 applied all over will ensure that you look great and stay safe. If by the pool, get a waterproof one and reapply as directed. If out doing sports, keep uncovered areas well protected. Reapply every two to three hours.

- Avoid the sun between eleven a.m. and three p.m. when it is at its strongest. If you can't avoid the sun, wear a hat and make sure your skin is well protected.

- When out in the sun, drink plenty of water to keep yourself hydrated. Dehydration makes your skin more vulnerable to the damaging and drying effects of the sun.

- Alternatively, there are loads of great fake tan products on the market so why sweat it in the sun?

Fake Tans

- For best results, don't be heavy-handed with fake tan. Additional layers can always be added later.
- Don't moisturize before applying fake tan.
- Exfoliate the area to be tanned before application.
- Don't apply fake tan to elbows or knee joints.
- Painted toenails look fantastic with tanned legs.

> Reading while sunbathing makes you well red.

Hair Care

Nothing looks better than a head of really shiny hair and yet some of the things we do—for example, blowdrying, coloring, bleaching and using cheap shampoos—can affect the condition of your hair, as can environmental factors (pollution and exposure to the sun and sea). However, there are ways to help your hair.

Oils for hair: As with the other areas of beauty, the essential oils can be added to your favorite brands of shampoo as this will boost their effectiveness and add that extra shine. Try rosemary, lavender, lemon, camomile, sandalwood, geranium, cedarwood. Remember you don't have to use all of them. You can use one with your favorite scent or a combination of a couple, e.g. rosemary and lemon.)

Top Tips for Hair

- Don't brush your hair immediately after you've washed it. Wrap your hair in a towel to soak up excess moisture and then brush once the towel is removed.
- Use shampoo suitable for your hair type.
- Use a conditioner suitable for your hair type.
- Use essential oils that are good for hair. Add a few drops to your shampoo or conditioner for a great shine whether your hair is dry or oily.

Dark hair: Rosemary and cedarwood.
Fair hair: Lemon and camomile.

- Have your hair trimmed every six weeks to get rid of split ends and to keep it generally healthy.
- For extra shine:

Dark hair: Add a tablespoon of vinegar to your rinse water.

Fair hair: Add the juice of half a lemon to your rinse water.

For Dandruff

- Use a shampoo especially for dandruff.
- Good essential oils to help prevent dandruff are rosemary, lemon, eucalyptus, or tea tree (very effective, but pongs a bit!) You can add a few drops to your shampoo, conditioner or rinse water.
- Sometimes cutting down on dairy products can help alleviate dandruff.

A Monthly Treatment

A lot of people ask Nesta how she keeps her hair looking like silk. This is her secret:

1. Add a drop of rosemary essential oil to a base oil (sunflower, olive, grape seed or almond).

2. Part the hair and apply the oil from the root of the hair to the ends.

3. Wrap your head in a warm towel and leave for fifteen minutes.

4. Shampoo thoroughly to remove all excess oil and you'll find that your hair is silky and glossy.

Using Essential Oils in Your Monthly Treatment

For greasy hair: Use 50ml base oil and add ten drops of lemon, rosemary or bergamot.

For dry hair: Use 50ml of base oil and add ten drops of sandalwood, camomile or lavender.

For normal hair: Use 50ml of base oil and ten drops of rosewood, lavender or rosemary.

Nails

Looking after your nails is simple. We all do manicures on each other when we do our DIY pampering sessions. Just follow these instructions and your hands will look fab.

- Keep nails clean.
- File them regularly. Follow the natural shape of the nail— if oval-shaped, file the nails like that, if a square shape, follow that.
- Push the cuticles back regularly. In the bath is a good time as the cuticles are soft and you don't have to force them.
- If you're going to paint your nails, keep the color fresh as nothing looks worse than chipped nails, especially if they're a dark color.
- Use hand cream regularly to keep the skin on your hands soft. Keep a tube or jar somewhere accessible so you remember.
- Stay away from false nails or nail extensions. The beauti-

cian at our local salon says that false nails can ruin the nail underneath and are very high maintenance.

- If you bite your nails, paint them in clear or in a pretty color and have regular manicures (or pedicures if you bite your toenails!). When they look nice, it will discourage you from biting them. Alternatively, ask at your local chemist for varnish to discourage nail biting. It tastes bitter and will soon put you off.

Hairy Bits
by Lucy

This is my area of personal expertise ever since I tried to wax my underarms at home. Big mistake, I can tell you, as it is the most painful thing I have ever ever lived through. Trouble was, I gaily applied the wax to both underarms and when I realized how agonizing it was to rip the wax off, I had to walk round with my arms up in the air until Mum got home and came to my rescue (and also had a good laugh along with the whole family). Anyway, some things are best left to the experts at the beauty salon. Others you can do painlessly and cheaply at home.

On the Face (Upper Lip and Chin)

It can feel really embarrassing to find that you're growing a fine moustache or have stray dark hairs on your upper lip and chin, but it is so common both with blondes and brunettes. Like a lot of darker skinned girls, Nesta found a few hairs on her chin and being the drama queen that she is, totally panicked as she thought she might be turning into a boy. As if. At first she made the mistake of plucking the hairs out, but then our local beautician told her that if anyone has any facial hair, plucking is not the answer as it strengthens the hair follicle. And don't shave it as it will grow back like stubble. Not a great look and certainly not a great sensation if up close and snogging a boy, as it's him who's supposed to give the snog rash, not the girl. Anyway, after Nesta came out about her hairy chin, TJ also admitted to being worried as she thought she was growing a moustache! She was so relieved to know she wasn't alone. There are several treatments available at beauty salons that are worth checking out for the removal of facial hair.

- If the hair on the upper lip is fine, but slightly dark and noticeable, a simple solution is to have the hair bleached.

Note from TJ: I had my "moustache" bleached and now no one notices it.

- Use a hair removing cream. This will dissolve the hair away and it will grow back softly (as opposed to stubbly).
- Electrolysis involves a course of treatment, but eventually, the removal of hair is permanent. A fine needle is injected into the hair root and zaps it with an electric current which destroys the hair follicle.

Note from Nesta: Arghhh. Whoever said you have to suffer to be beautiful was dead right in this case!

- Epil pro also involves a course of treatment over a few years, but can also have permanent results. It is a lot less painful than electrolysis and works by using high-pitched sound waves to eliminate hair growth.

Note from Nesta: It feels like having the hairs tweezed out really quickly and is absolutely bearable, even for a wimp like me.

- Laser. A wavelength of light is used to destroy the hair follicles. It can be expensive, but hair removal is permanent and pain is minimal. Although, some places claim that only one treatment is needed, while others say that most people need between two to six sessions so check your finances and what your local clinic charges before committing.

Note from Nesta: I couldn't afford this one, but will have it done when I am rich and famous.

On the Eyebrows
- Don't go mad and pluck them into a thin line.
- Do pluck in the middle if you have one eyebrow instead of two.
- Never shave them.

- Follow the natural curve of your brow. Never try to change the shape of your eyebrows. Just clean up any hairs between and below your two brows

- Carefully brush eyebrows upward, then trim off excess hair above the natural arch of your eyebrow.

- Avoid pain during eyebrow plucking by placing an ice cube on the area for fifteen seconds before plucking.

- Pluck your eyebrows before bedtime so any redness will disappear overnight.

- Pull the stray hairs out in the direction of the ears.

- If uncertain, have it done in a salon by a beautician and follow the lines she does when you do it at home.

On the Legs

- Go hairy. Wahey. But we don't think this is a great look—especially in the summer when you've got a short dress on.

- Shaving: Cheap and fast, but the hair grows back quickly and can get stubbly. It's okay for underarms, though.

- Waxing: this is the method we all use for our legs. With regular waxing, the hair takes between four to six weeks to reappear so you don't have to think about it for ages and the regrowth is soft. If you can't afford to have it done at a salon, there are lots of home kits on sale at most chemist's and you can make it part of your beautifying session. Offer to do it for one of your mates if she's annoyed you! For underarms, get it done at a salon as it is way to painful to attempt at home (see my note at the beginning of this section).

NB: Waxing or hair removal (such as electrolysis) always feels more painful when you have your period so try to schedule hair removal sessions for other times of the month.

Braces

Nesta has braces and although she hates them, we all think she still looks fab. So here's what we think:

- It's going to be well worth it in the long run when you have picture-perfect pegs.
- Just about everyone wears them at some point or other these days. It's no biggie any more. Don't hide behind your hands. Take the "love me, love my braces" attitude and wear then with pride! Think of them as a fashion accessory. Some people wear metal in their ears, you wear it on your teeth. Cool.

Note from Nesta: When snuggling into a boy's neck or shoulder, if he's wearing anything made of wool, keep your mouth shut or you might (like I did once) get caught up in his sweater.

Health

Dieting

We thought we'd also hand this section over to TJ's mum as she's a doctor and knows a lot about dieting sensibly, as opposed to all Izzie's mad methods of starvation that don't work because she always puts the weight back on immediately when she can't keep it up!

To Diet or Not to Diet
by Dr. Watts

It can seem really unfair to be a person who's prone to putting on weight. Some girls can eat what they like and never put on an ounce, whereas others feel that they have only to look at food and it goes to their hips, legs, or tummy. A lot of teens who feel that they are overweight are actually completely normal, but sadly telling them that doesn't help—especially if their best friend is a skinny thing with a flat abdomen permanently on show. Before you embark on a weight loss program, first you have to ask yourself, are you *really* overweight or are you striving to look like some model in a magazine? If you really feel that you do need to shift some weight, here's the best way to go about it:

- Forget fad diets. Any diet that promises that you'll drop a stone in a few weeks won't work in the long run and you'll put the weight back on. Sorry, but it's true, and in the case of a lot of diets that do cause you to drop five pounds quickly, it's usually only water you lose. If you're serious about losing weight and keeping it off, more often than not it has to be a lifestyle change and you have to completely rethink how and what you eat. You probably didn't put the weight you want to lose on in two weeks—it was the culmination of years of your eating habits. In the same way, you're not going to lose the weight in two weeks. You have to look at permanent weight loss as a long-term thing. A loss of between one to two pounds a week is a sensible rate of loss that should be easier to maintain.

- Up your activity. Look at your lifestyle. If you sit at school most of the day, get a lift home, then blob in front of a computer or the TV, it's no wonder that you are gaining weight. Try to do some activity for at least 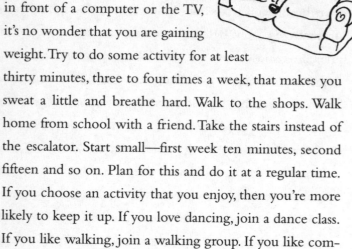 thirty minutes, three to four times a week, that makes you sweat a little and breathe hard. Walk to the shops. Walk home from school with a friend. Take the stairs instead of the escalator. Start small—first week ten minutes, second fifteen and so on. Plan for this and do it at a regular time. If you choose an activity that you enjoy, then you're more likely to keep it up. If you love dancing, join a dance class. If you like walking, join a walking group. If you like competitive sport, play tennis or squash and so on. The positive side to regular exercise is that you can still have the occasional treat as you'll burn it off, if you get off your behind.
- Be realistic. How much do you need to lose? For realistic body shapes, look around you at the mall and at school. Don't look at models on TV or in magazines. It's amazing what airbrushing, lighting and camera tricks can do to lengthen legs and reduce hips.
- Don't panic and stop eating. You really don't have to suffer

or deny yourself to look good. Starvation will make you look and feel ill which goes against why you're trying to lose weight— to look better. You will look your best if you eat a sensible, healthy diet and are active.

- Change your eating habits. Losing weight doesn't mean deprivation. Doctors have found that cutting down what you eat isn't always the answer, but *changing* what you eat can be. Replace fatty foods, refined foods and fast foods with fresh food, fruit, vegetables and eat wholemeal bread instead of white and you'll soon see results. (Also, many refined foods have added flavour that makes you want to eat more of them.)

- Let your family know that you're serious about losing some weight so that you have their support and won't feel like you have to do it in secret. Hopefully, they'll make dietary changes that will help the whole family and if your parents buy plenty of foods that you can eat you won't be tempted to hit the biscuit tin.

- Forget diet pills that offer to burn the fat off or speed up your metabolism. The only way to lose weight and keep it off is to combine a healthy diet with exercise. If your metabolism has become sluggish from sitting around, regular exercise will help it pick up.

- Don't skip breakfast. Have something healthy like fruit, grains, wholemeal bread or yogurt. Overnight, your metabolism slows down and eating something gets it going again and will prevent you from feeling starving mid-morning.

- Get into the habit of drinking water or sugar-free drinks instead of fizzy drinks that are loaded with sugar and calories. Switch from full fat milk to skimmed milk.

- Don't be hard on yourself if you overeat one day. Get back on track the next day.

- If out and there's nothing you can eat but fattening food, have a little and load up on vegetables if there are any.

- Join a slimming club. There are local clubs everywhere and they usually advocate a sensible diet where you won't feel deprived and will lose weight gradually, rather than a mad fad quick fix that offers unrealistic losses and ultimately doesn't work. At the clubs, you can get the support of other members who are trying to lose weight, get loads of brilliant advice and recipes, plus the weekly weigh-in means that you can't kid yourself if you're not sticking to it.

- If you're really worried that nothing is working, see your doctor. He or she will be able to size up your body shape in relation to your height, weight and age and tell you what weight you should be for you.

Note from Izzie: And it sometimes helps to stick a photo of yourself at your fattest on the fridge door to remind yourself of how you got that way! Make sure you remove it, when a cool boy is coming round, though.

And so, your hair is looking great, your skin is glowing, your brace is sparkling, your acne has taken a hike. Here are a few more tips to help you look your best.

Eating to Survive and Thrive
by Mr. Lovering (Lucy's dad)

Of course eating is essential for survival, but what you eat can make the difference between merely surviving or thriving. You can eat badly and feel crapola or eat healthily and feel great. The choice is yours and this part is over to Lucy's dad, Mr. Lovering, for some good guidelines as he runs the local health shop and knows what's what and what's not.

> Practise safe eating—
> always use condiments!

You are what you eat may be a cliché, but the fact is that your basic diet has a tremendous effect on not only how you look, but how you feel. If you have been experiencing fatigue, sluggishness or stress, it can be remedied by changing your dietary habits. If you eat rubbish, you can often end up feeling that way. If you're not getting the proper nutrients from your food, you're not going to have the energy to function to your maximum potential and can feel like you're "running on empty." If you eat the right foods, you'll feel more vibrant, look better and have more energy.

Just bear in mind the following principles and you'll be on your way to better health and energy levels:

- Eat plenty of fresh produce. Fruit and vegetables, at least five portions a day (organic if you can get it).
- Drink a litre of water a day, two if you can manage it.

- Cut out or reduce all refined foods, e.g. white flour products such as pasta, bread, biscuits and cake. Replace with whole grains, wholemeal bread and pasta, brown rice and pulses. If you want biscuits and cakes, either bake them at home with wholemeal flour and unrefined sugar or buy produce with natural ingredients.

- Cut out fast foods/junk foods that contain preservatives, coloring and additives, and replace with homemade meals from fresh produce.

- Reduce fatty foods and replace with baked or grilled foods.

- Reduce your salt intake.

- Reduce your sugar intake.

- Keep coffee to a maximum of two cups a day.

- A little bit of what you fancy does no harm every now and then, i.e. in moderation.

- Make sure you're getting enough calcium in your diet for healthy bone development. Sources of calcium are dairy products and some bread.

- If you're feeling tired or sluggish, ensure you're getting enough iron and protein in your diet. Sources of iron are meat, fish, eggs, green leafy vegetables and breakfast cereals. Sources of protein are meat, fish, eggs, nuts and beans or pulses. If you're unsure, you can ask your doctor to do a test for anaemia, which can make you tired and pale and can be caused by an iron deficiency.

And there you have it—good health!

Going Organic
by Izzie Foster

When it comes to my soul, I don't know
I've got questions without any answers
But in the fight for my body I'm in control
I want my food from the earth not a chemical plant
When it comes to taste it's a real tough choice
I'm just a happy eater who dreams of pizza
And when it comes to health food I'm just a big cheater
I am what I eat, but junks got me beat
Gotta eat better, be a real trend-setter, a healthy go-getter
Cut out the burgers, kick out chocs
I don't want to end up fat in a wooden box
Must eat organic and save the planet
But I'm a happy eater who dreams of pizza
And when it comes to health food I'm just a big cheater

Fashion by LL

(i.e. Lucy Lovering of
Lucy Lovering Designs)

Bras

Starting, ahem, with the undergarment. Gawd knows why the girls are letting me do this section as I have no chest to speak of, although it has grown *slightly* in the last year. (And I mean slightly, you still need a microscope!) However, as I design my own clothes and want my own label when I leave school, I have learned how important the right bra is. It can totally improve your shape. However, shopping for bras can be a daunting experience.

The problem: There are so many types these days that it can be hard to know where to start. Not just colors and fabrics, but types: bras for total support, ego-boosters, minimisers, bras with no front, no back, no straps, balcony bras, wired, plunge, moulded, padded, seamed, non-padded, five-way, sheer, halter neck, cross-over, one shoulder, bioform, sculptured, push-up, multiway, T-shirt, sport, stretch and many more. It's no wonder we get confused and it can be easy just to grab one that looks about right and leave it at that. Apparently, though, seven in ten girls wear the wrong size for their shape.

The solution: Most large stores now have an in-house measuring service so you can make sure that you are wearing the right fit. It's really worth taking the time to get this done—the right bra under outfits can totally improve your shape and stops that horrible riding up at the back or puckering around the cup that you can get if you're wearing the wrong size. When you have established your size, try on a few different designs in the same size as some will look better than others, some make you look pointy, others push you up or flatten you and so on.

Clothes

It's so easy to go shopping and end up with a wardrobe stuffed with clothes that don't go with anything else or were an impulse buy. Regardless of what your style is, there are certain items that every girl should have in her wardrobe.

The Essential Wardrobe
(for Girlie or Goth)

- One pair of well-fitting jeans. These can be worn for casual wear or dressed up with a sparkly top for evening. When shopping for these, take a friend (like Nesta) who will give you an honest opinion of how you look in them from behind!
- One pair of black trousers, as they make you look slim and go with anything.
- One flirty skirt. Skirts cut on the bias are the most flattering.

143

- One sparkly or glam top for the evening. It can be worn with trousers, jeans or a skirt.
- One jacket. Again, take an honest friend with you when you shop for this as different cuts look good on different shapes.
- A big comfy sweater or sweatshirt to cover you up on days when you're feeling bloated.
- A coat. Single-breasted is the most flattering.
- One good T-shirt (you can't go wrong with white).
    - One pair of killer high heels. If you have thicker legs, stay away from ankle straps as they make legs look shorter and ankles look bigger.
    - One pair of trainers for when you have to walk a lot.

To these essential items you can add your own preferences in tops, accessories and you're away, looking good!

Lucy's Top Tips for Making the Most of Yourself

- Stand up straight. Don't slouch or hunch over. Think "supermodel" and strut your stuff.

- Eat fresh, healthy food. As mentioned previously, hair and skin glow on a good diet and are dull on a stodgy junk food diet. You are what you eat (though the occasional choc fest is absolutely permissable).

- Have regular pampering sessions, even if they're DIY at home. You'll get the idea that you're worth it, and others will pick up on this.

- Pay attention to details: nails, hands, feet, eyebrows, skin.

- Keep hair clean and well cut. It's Murphy's Law—the day you put off washing your hair is the day you'll bump into someone you fancy, so be prepared.

- Save up and buy one wonderful item that makes you feel fabulous whenever you put it on.

- Wear underwear that fits properly and looks good (see later section on how to get the right bra fit).

- Think positively. Of all things you wear, your expression is that one that people see first so smile, it's the best beauty aid there is. If you are miserable and bored with yourself, others will pick up on that.

- Invest in a pair of fab sunglasses for days when you feel tired and not at your best.

- Ninety percent of looking good comes from confidence. Believe in yourself. Everyone has it in them to look wonderful in their own individual way. Find out what suits you. A designer label doesn't guarantee the item will look fab on you. (If you're not sure what your style is, most of the big stores now have personal shoppers. You book an appointment and after an initial short consultation with you, they will scour the store on your behalf and bring back a load of fab outfits for you to try. It's usually a free service and there's no obligation to buy anything they bring if you don't like it.)

PART THREE
Survival Tips for Every Occasion

by TJ Watts

The girls asked me (TJ) to coordinate this part because, as you'll see, a number of different people have contributed. In this day and age, there's more to being cool than just wearing the right outfit. It pays for a girl to be street smart as well as beautiful so this next section is about about survival at school, at home and out and about—and how to get through some of the situations that arise for us teens. It's best to be in the know where you can. As the boy scouts say, Be prepared.

Surviving at School

Dealing with Bullies
by Nesta Williams

People who know me now think that I am mega confident and good at seeing bullies off, but I wasn't always like this. I was bullied at my last school and it's an experience I'll never forget. Why they picked on me, I don't really know.

Maybe they were jealous, maybe they didn't like the way I looked, maybe the sound of my voice irritated them. Who knows? There are just some mean people out there who can make life miserable for the rest of us. They've probably got problems of their own which makes them take it out on those who appear weaker or different. One thing I do know, though, is that no one deserves to be a punch bag or dumping ground for someone else's problems. At first I thought it must be me—my fault—that there was something wrong with me, then one day I realized, No, I'm okay, actually—it's them who've got the problem and I don't want to be part of it. Eventually I did learn to stand up for myself and I've put some of the ways I learned to deal with bullies down below.

First of all, how do you recognise that you're being bullied? It's not always physical. Bullying can take many forms:

- Teasing
- Name-calling

- Humiliating
- Excluding
- Ignoring
- Physical violence
- Stealing from
- Spreading rumours

Here's what to do if any of the above are happening to you or someone you know:

- Where possible, avoid situations when you might be alone with the bully. This isn't being cowardly—why walk into trouble if you can avoid it?
- If you can't avoid situations where the bullies hang out or if you fear a certain route or place, make sure that you're accompanied when you go there.
- As far as you can, don't show that you're upset. If bullies don't get a reaction, they'll soon lose interest.
- If you are threatened with violence over money or possessions, hand them over without a fight, as your safety is more important, then let an adult know as soon as possible. This isn't snitching. No one has the right to nick your stuff and make you miserable.

- Speak up for yourself. I know it can be hard if you're shy or lacking in confidence, but you have every right to go to school or about your everyday business without being hassled. If someone is giving you a hard time, don't just take it. Talk back, stick up for yourself and if you can't handle it by yourself, let someone know who can help you, whether it be friends, family or teachers. If someone dismisses your problem or is unhelpful, choose to move on and find someone who does take you seriously. Many teens don't want to tell a teacher as they fear it will only worsen the situation. You and your friends could, however, ask a teacher to set up a box where people can leave anonymous notes letting them know what is going on. Bullying needs to be brought to a school's attention and can be stopped. And often they don't want to tell a parent for fear of them causing a fuss by charging in to sort the situation out—in which case, you could always ask them to slow down and discuss solutions first. Remember that the bully needs help too and if the situation is brought to light, you will also be helping other prospective victims as well as the bully (bullying behaviour can stem from unhappiness, lack of self esteem and sometimes they've even been bullied themselves and they're taking it out on someone else).

- Don't be a victim. Don't go into "poor me" consciousness and let bullies walk all over you, like they're the strong ones and you're the weak one. Act like a person that no one would ever bully. Walk tall and confidently. Look people in the eye. Be ASSERTIVE.

- Take a self-defence course. Not so that you can to engage in a fight, but just knowing that you can defend yourself will improve your confidence.

- If you're not ready to speak to anyone, go to the library and look at books there written about how to deal with bullying. Alternatively there are many good sites on the internet that also deal with it. Just type "bullying" into your search engine.

- You do have choices. You can choose to change things. It may feel that you have no control at all and are totally at the mercy of someone else's nastiness. Not true. You always have a choice as to how you are going to *deal* with a situation and choosing to be a victim and letting the situation carry on is only *one* of those choices. Other choices are to do something about it and if you can't handle it alone, choose to get help. Bullying is not something that is happening only to you. It has happened all over the world to thousands of people and if you don't want to tell your parents or teachers, there are other people and organisations equipped to deal with it, such as ChildLine which is a confidential twenty-four hour phone line that you can call if in trouble (0800 11 11 or www.childline.org.uk) You're not alone. You may feel as if you are, but often people stay silent because of fear. You will be doing everyone a big favor if you help the situation to be dealt with.

Good luck. Remember all the clichés. The darkest hour is just before dawn, etc., etc. There was a time when I was so miserable that I felt my life was over and I'd never be happy again. All because of some mean-spirited kids. I got through it and if you're being bullied, I know that you can too.

Studying

Study Tips
by Mrs. Allen

Ever wondered how some teens get good results at school? Not always because they're natural brainboxes and clever things just pour out of them like water out of a tap. Nope. It's because they've got their study time sorted. This is hot of the press from our headteacher, Mrs. Allen, so pay attention as she can be very strict!

Preparation

- If possible, have a specific place to study where there are no distractions and you have space to lay out your books.

- Turn off the TV and ask your family to hold your calls. Turn off your mobile.

- Time-manage. A reasonable amount each day works better than last minute panic-cramming as you have so much to take in. Prepare a timetable of revision and stick to it!

- Choose a regular time each day for your study. That way, your mind will come to recognise the time for home-work or revising and be more receptive.

- Make a checklist of what needs to be done so that you can see that you are progressing.

- Don't try to work too late at night.

- Always make sure you've a number of good quality pens you are used to using.

- Effective working means setting yourself clear and realistic goals both in the short-term and the long-term. Don't try to read all the set books in one short period! Once again, time-manage.

- Be clear about what you need to do. For example: some-times there is no need to read *every* book closely. Some are for reference, some can be scanned with concentration only on selected parts. Some books require careful study. Your teacher should give you guidance on this.

- Make sure you have the books you need, such as a home dictionary.

Attitude

- Don't put off until tomorrow what you can do today. And the sooner your work is done, the sooner you can catch that movie or whatever it is you want to do. Plus you'll enjoy your leisure time more as you won't have that homework hanging over you.

- Take responsibility for organising your own studies and don't be dependent on teachers to organise every little thing for you. This means not leaving study to the last minute.

- Set realisable targets and plan rewards for when you meet them.

- Ignore people who appear to be successful without revising; it's rarely true.

- Learn to say "no" to your friends who keep ringing up or want you to come out. Your boyfriend will have to put up with seeing you only twice a week.

Looking After Yourself

- Include fresh air and physical exercise in your revision regime to keep your head clear.

- Don't skip meals. Eat fresh, nutritious food as opposed to junk or fast food. Fish oils are also reputed to help brain power so eat oily fish (such as salmon) or take fish oil capsules (such as cod liver oil).

- Make sure your desk and chair are at a good height for you to prevent back- or neckache.

- Take a short break every now and then to stretch, get a drink or give yourself a reward.

- Expect a modicum of anxiety. It can be a good thing since it means you are motivated. Over-anxiety is usually the result of letting work and tasks pile up until you feel engulfed.

- Adequate sleep is extremely important, so have some early nights—especially around exam times.

- Schedule some leisure time so that your brain has time to rest and take in all your studying.

Revision

- Don't keep putting revision off—the closer you are to an exam the more stressed you will be and the less effectively you will revise.

- Make revision cards—they can be useful as a ready reminder on the bus to school.

- Talk about your work with others studying the same subjects. It helps you to remember it and alerts you to anything you need to revisit that you're struggling to explain.

- Put posters of key formulas and quotes around your bedroom, on the fridge, etc.

- Revision is like fitness-training: the more you do the more you can do.

- Use different color highlighter pens for important points in different areas.

- Prepare bullet point responses to past exam questions (your teacher can usually provide these).

- Read through your notes at different speeds. It helps sometimes just to flick through them to remind yourself of what's there.

- Use travel time to catch up on reading.

- And Izzie may be surprised to see this one, but she's not the only one who knows her essential oils! Basil and peppermint essential oil both have properties than sharpen the concentration and aid memory so can be used to help in study time. Put a few drops on a tissue and inhale when you feel like your head is overstuffed with facts and your mind is growing fuzzy and weary.

Exams

- Wear layers on the day of exams so you can wrap up or peel off and be optimally comfortable.

- Make sure you have all you need in the way of pens, pencils, water and so on.

- Don't drink lots of coffee to wake yourself up—you'll spend half the exam busting to go to the loo.

- Prepare your answers to exam questions during the exam because when examiners see evidence of planning (outlines/notes) they anticipate superior responses, but make it clear what is your answer and what is your rough planning.

- Avoid crossing out work in exams. Every year perfectly good responses that have been crossed out cannot be credited.

- Read exam questions carefully and ensure you respond to all aspects of it, e.g. if it says "to what extent" or "how far do you agree" you MUST discuss both sides of the argument/evidence and come to a balanced conclusion.
- Do your best in the exam, come out and forget all about it . . .

Education Rap
by Izzie Foster

Now I'm walkin' down the street with my feet on the beat
An' I look real cool cos I ain't no fool, I go to school
Don't wanna be a loser, a street corner boozer, a bum for rum
or a no hope dope
Now I'm really going places, I'm holdin' all aces
I got smart cos I know in my heart I got real good start
I'm ahead of the pack, no lookin' back, I'm goin' up, don't
need no luck
Cos I ain't no fool I go to school . . .

Excuses
by Lal Lovering

This is the part that Lal is blackmailing us to put in. He says
that if we don't, he's going to put photos of Lucy aged five,
wearing her dinner on her head, on the Internet. We've seen
the pics. Mashed potato and peas in the hair is not a good look
so we have no choice, but to let Lal go ahead. I guess they may

come in useful when you've totally failed at putting into practice any of the study tips, you haven't done your homework or revision. Er . . . some you may find more useful than others!

Excuses for Handing in Homework Late

1. My homework is late because I was up all night writing letters demanding better pay for teachers.
2. I couldn't do my homework because I accidentally superglued my teeth together and had to go to the dentist.
3. I couldn't do my homework because my contact lenses stuck to my eyes.
4. I *have* done my homework, but it's done in invisible ink.
5. My homework's late because I have an attention deficit disorder, er . . . what was I saying?

Excuses for Being Late to School

1. I'm late because a giant centipede ran off with all my shoes.
2. I'm late because I woke up in a parallel universe and it was two hours earlier there.
3. I was here on time, but I had an invisibility attack and you didn't see me.

4. I'm haven't been in lately as I'm becoming a vampire and can't go out in the daylight.

5. I'm late because a power cut during the night stopped my alarm clock.

6. I'm late because someone stole the wheels off my bike (only use this one if you do have a bike).

7. I'm late because God wanted to talk to me. Again.

(**Note from the girls:** Lal obviously has a very vivid imagination for excuses and we suggest a career in politics. And somehow we don't think Mrs. Allen would buy a lot of these excuses!)

> Voice over the phone: Johnny Dickens won't be in today.
> Teacher: Who is this speaking?
> Voice: This is my father speaking . . .

Advanced Class Excuses

Visual aids to use as excuses:

1. Invest in a broken watch, then say, that can't be the time!

2. Buy stick on spots and say you're coming down with something nasty. Everyone will believe you. Same goes for white or pale green makeup.

3. Buy some diced mixed vegetables. Before arriving home, take a mouthful, but don't swallow. When you see your parent, spit out vegetables and groan. They'll think you've thrown up. Guaranteed sympathy.

4. Get yourself a leg cast, then as you limp in you can say, "Sorry bit of an accident!"

5. Buy a rubber cat. You can just hold it up and say, "Found this in the road, got to report it to the vet and find it's owner."

Super Advanced Excuses!

If someone rings your doorbell and you're not sure if you want to spend time with them, put your coat on when you answer. If you like them, you can say, "Oh I've just got in" and take your coat off. If you don't you can say, "Oh I'm just going out" and walk them to the gate.

And sometimes you'll need an excuse for having acted crazy.

We all have days when we say mad things or act in an unusual way. Here's how to get explain yourself.

1. "Aliens landed and took over my brain for two hours."
2. "No! That wasn't me. That was my psychotic twin. We don't usually let her out, but she escaped last night for a short while. Soooooo sorreeeeeeeeeeeeeee."
3. Say you're an actress: "I was researching a role for my new movie where I have to play a mad girl and I wanted to get into the character for a while."

Surviving at Home

Sometimes, us teenagers can be vastly misunderstood and these times can lead to parents feeling that they need to make a point and punish us. Being grounded seems to be a popular choice for punishments, so here's how to get through it if it happens to you. As Izzie seems to be the one grounded most often, I asked her to do this section!

Things to Do When You're Grounded

- Catch up on homework. (Yuck, but it *is* an option and can buy brownie points with your parents when you get a stunning report card.)

- Color coordinate your wardrobe for easy access.

- Store shoes in boxes. Take Polaroids/digital photos of the shoes and stick them on the outside of the box for quick identification.

- Do some feng shui on your bedroom and get rid of all the clutter. If you haven't worn something for over a year, take it to a charity shop.

- Line drawers with scented paper to keep clothes smelling fresh.

- Update your address book. Then update your diary.

- Feng shui your computer (tidy desktop and clear up old files).

- Start your bestselling novel. If grounded for a loooong time, also finish it.

- Try moving all your furniture around for a new look.

- Redecorate your room.

- Learn to meditate.
- Do your Christmas card list and plan presents.
- Check out astrology sites on the Web and do friends' horoscopes.
- Treat the time like being in a health spa: give yourself a facial, paint your nails, condition your hair, moisturize and exfoliate your skin.
- Exercise.
- Listen to music.
- Write music or lyrics.
- Learn to cook a new recipe (earns good brownie points if it comes out well and may get you time off for good behaviour).
- Clean the house and do the garden (also earns brownie points).
- Read. Books are cool and it's a great way to escape from your personal prison into other worlds.

Dealing With Parents

(also by Iz)

N

Planet Parent

S

Dealing with parents can sometimes be a minefield as they seem to speak a different language to the rest of the planet. There was a time when I really didn't get on with my mum and would barely speak to my step dad—in fact I used to call him the Lodger as I couldn't get my head round the fact that he really was living with us. We get on great now (well most of the time, my mum can be way uptight sometimes), but we've learned to talk and that helps a lot. All of us have times when we love and then loathe our parents and they love and then loathe us so here a few tips for getting through the bad times:

- Remember that they didn't get a manual when you were born and sometimes (often) make mistakes.

- Keep communicating. If something's bothering you, let them know as sometimes they can surprise you and be helpful.

- Let them know where you are or if you're going to be late. They do worry and are a lot nicer to deal with if you keep them in the loop.

- Remember their birthdays and let them know from time

to time that you appreciate them.

- And a good tip I picked up from Nesta is to always show your report card to them when they're either on the phone or watching their favorite TV show. That way they're distracted!

C'mon Let's Dance
by Izzie Foster

My mother is a hippie,
My stepdad is a geek,
My friends all play video games seven days a week.
I'm stuck in the middle, what else can I say?
We're all just little kids, though some of us are grey.
So let's dance, c'mon everybody, let's dance.

You're a short time growing up
And a very long time dead
Sometimes you gotta shake the serious
Right outta your head.
So let's dance, c'mon everybody, let's dance.

So grab yourself a hippie, hang on to a freak.
Put your loudest music on and get up on your feet.
And let's dance, c'mon everybody, let's dance.
Let's dance, c'mon everybody, let's dance.

> Insanity is hereditary.
> You get it from your kids.

Here are a few of the common phrases parents use and an explanation of what they actually mean:

Parent-Speak

When I was your age . . .

What's this lying on the floor?

What It Means

Prepare for a lecture about how, when they were your age, they were a lot better behaved.

It's yours. Pick it up immediately.

We need to have a "word".   Prepare for a telling off

That TV programme doesn't look very interesting.   Turn it off. 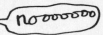 nooooooo

It's getting late.   Go to bed.

Your room's a mess.   Tidy it up, RIGHT NOW.

Are you watching this TV programme?   Turn over. I want to watch something else.

It's time you learned to look after yourself as I won't be around for ever.   Wash up

Maybe.   No.

I'll think about it.   No.

Ask me later.   No.

Ask your father.   . . . who will say no

We need to talk.   I need to complain / You've done something wrong.

You must learn to communicate.   You must learn to agree with me.

Go ahead (with raised eyebrow).   This is not permission, it is a dare! Be careful.

Go ahead (normal eyebrows).   I give up. (Still be careful, though, as parent may change their mind.)

Loud sigh.

Although not verbal, this means why are they wasting their time on you?

My mum does bird imitations.
She watches me like a hawk.

Dealing With Siblings
by Lucy

Let's face it, older and younger brothers and sisters can be a pain. They nick your things, invade your space (especially my brother  Steve) and humiliate you in public (my brother Lal). Yet you're stuck with them at least until you leave home. Here are some handy hints for making life easier:

- Respect their space. They have a right to live at your house too.
- Don't borrow their stuff without asking. This includes clothes, CDs, cameras, videos, and books.
- Always leave the bathroom how you'd like to find it.
- Don't hog the bathroom.
- Knock before you enter their bedroom.

- Write down messages from their mates if they're not in and leave them where your sibling can see them.
- Make sure you all do your share of household chores. This can be negotiated with parents.
- Negotiate an equal share of what TV programmes are to be watched. (This means giving them their pick every now and again!)
- Ditto re: use of the computer.
- Be supportive of one another in stressful times such as relationship break-ups, exams and so on.
- Bother to find out what the problem is if they're acting unusually moody or bad tempered.

Out and About

Surviving Social Occasions
by Cressida Forbes

First of all, let me say how flattered I am to have been asked to do this section on social etiquette. I've decided to keep it general as accepted behaviour can vary from culture to culture—however, there are certain things that will help you be successful in society wherever you are and whoever you're with.

- Always RSVP if an invite asks you to.

- In social situations, learn to listen as well as talk. Sometimes when people are nervous, they gabble away and don't give the person they're talking to a chance to say a word. A good conversationalist talks and listens equally.

- Don't be late for any engagement, especially if meeting in a public place. It says: Your time doesn't matter and mine is more important. To be late is disrespectful.

- When eating out or at a dinner party, knives and forks are to be used in order, from the outside in, so start with the ones furthest away from your plate. If you're skipping a starter, use the largest inside knife and fork for your main course.

- Finger bowls are for washing your fingers in when given something like prawns or seafood. Not for drinking from.

- Pot pourri is to scent the room. It is not a snack.

- Place your napkin on your lap, not tucked in at your neck.

- Close your mouth when you eat. Take small bites and don't shove food in your face all at once.

- Don't cut all your food up at once. You're not a baby.

- Twirl pasta on to your fork—don't slurp it up.

- Spoon soup and tilt the bowl away from you. Don't pick up the bowl and drink from it.

- If you have dietary requirements, let your hostess know in advance.

- Don't start eating until the hostess does or she tells everyone to go ahead and eat.

- Don't speak with your mouth full. Not everyone wants to see your mushed up broccoli, thank you very much.

- When finished, position your knife and fork parallel to each other at an angle across your plate.

- If at a dinner party and your host or hostess serves something you don't like, don't act like a princess and say you can't/won't eat it (unless it's something like a camel's eye or sheep's testicle in which case you can maybe say something like you're allergic to them). Try and eat a little. Or eat what you can, e.g. the vegetables (and if no one's looking, feed what you can't eat to the dog, tip it into a pot plant or wrap it in a napkin and put it in your bag.)

- At parties, introduce guests who don't know anyone to other guests.

- Send a thank-you card after a formal dinner or party. At more casual events, it's still nice to get a phone call or e-mail saying you enjoyed it.

- Don't talk during a film at the cinema. You're not at home with your mates and not everyone wants to hear your running commentary on the movie, no matter how brilliant your observations are.

- Always send thank-you cards or an e-mail or make a phone call to say thank you if someone has sent you a gift. Even if you don't like it.

Note from Nesta: As if we didn't know all this!

TJ's Tips for Being Streetwise

- If you have a mobile, always keep a taxi number in your phone menu for times of emergency or times you can't reach someone you know. Try to wait somewhere public until the taxi arrives.

- Walk confidently with purpose—head up, briskly.

- If out at night, try to always travel in a group.

- Trust your intuition. If you get a bad feeling about a place or a person, that's your intuition telling you to be careful.

- Keep your keys in your pocket in case someone tries to steal your bag—that way at least you can get in your front door.

- If you ever feel you're being followed, cross the street and see if whoever's following does the same. If they do, get to a populated area as fast as possible and keep your mobile within reach, but out of sight. Head for a police station, shop, service station or other public area. If necessary, yell to bring attention to the fact that you are being pursued.

- It's a good idea to have a bag that you can strap diagonally across your body—it's harder for someone to grab it and run.

- Don't walk in dark, secluded places or take shortcuts when there's an alternative route. Use routes home that are well-lit where there are still people about, even if it means walking further.

- Be aware of places in which people could hide, such as alleyways, bushes and on staircases.

- Don't make eye contact with strangers.

- It's not a great idea to wear a personal stereo when out walking or jogging as you can't hear if anyone approaches or comes up behind you (or traffic, for that matter).

- Never hesitate to call and ask someone to pick you up, even if it's late.

- Never accept a lift from a stranger. If a stranger ever asks if you want a lift, always say no and that your dad is on his way and will be there any minute. Then immediately phone the person you know who lives nearest and ask them to come and get you.

- In bars or clubs, keep an eye on your drink or always keep it in your hand. Don't accept drinks from strangers as sometimes they can be spiked.

- If travelling on the Tube, always travel in a compartment with people in it. If they get off at a stop, leaving the carriage empty, get off with them and get into another carriage with people in.

- If ever you are mugged for personal property, don't fight. Hand over your phone, watch or purse, then leg it.

- If ever a suspicious stranger approaches you on the bus, Tube or in the street and touches you or starts to engage, say *loudly*, "I don't know you, please go away." This will alert people around to the fact that the person is a stranger and it's not some private encounter.

- Remember 911 is the emergency number for ambulances, police and fire stations.

- It's a good idea to do a self-defense class. It will build your confidence as you'll know that you can defend yourself should the need arise. Your gym teacher will probably know where you could go to study.

- If you are attacked, you could try these moves:

  1. If approached from the front, kick the attacker in the shins or groin (straight up between the legs) or jab their eyes or throat.

  2. If attacked from behind, stomp on the attacker's foot with your heel, kick backward—aiming for the

groin—knee or elbow the attacker in the head, throat or the area between the ribcage and stomach.

3. Use your voice (make as much noise as possible to scare the attacker and attract attention), hands and feet. If picked up, kick with your legs to resist.

4. Once you're free, leg it as fast as you can and get help.

Things to Do if You Get Stranded With No Dosh

- Call someone you know, if you have a mobile.
- If you don't have your mobile, call someone you know from a public phone and reverse the charges.
- Get a cab to someone or somewhere you know. Get them to pay the cab fare at their end, then settle up with them later.
- Ask a police officer for help.

Surviving Financially:
Managing the Dosh

We thought this section was a bit of a joke as none of us really has a lot of finance to manage. However, Izzie's mother, Mrs. Foster, who works as an accountant, insists that there are a few things we ought to know, so over to her.

£££, $$$—Or Lack of It
by Mrs. Foster

Learning to manage your money early on will stand you in good stead as an adult. Lack or mismanagement of finances can be one of the major causes of stress when older and if handled badly, money is one of the major reasons for divorce. You're never too young to learn some good habits!

- Learn to budget. Make a list of the things that you want and what they cost, what expenses you have coming up, e.g. friends' birthdays/Christmas presents, etc, and make a realistic spending and savings plan.

- Be clear with your parents about exactly what your pocket money is supposed to cover and stick to what's agreed.

- Keep an account of how much money you have and what you've spent.

- Save a little every week for an emergency fund. It soon adds up and it's a good feeling to know that you have a stash put by for emergencies (such as a new must-have outfit, book or lipstick).

- Pay off any debts before making new purchases.

- Don't expect your parents to fork out for everything as they don't have an endless supply of money. If you want something badly and your parents can't afford it, think about getting a part-time job or asking around to see if anyone wants a babysitter. It gives you a great feeling to earn your own money and, to a certain degree, to be financially independent.

I want cards for my birthday.
Visa, American Express, Mastercard . . .

PART FOUR
Relaxation and Fun Time

by ??????

Things to Do on a Rainy Day
(Or Sunny. Or Windy.)

We've all worked on this section and decided to start with a bit of redecorating! Your bedroom is your own personal chill-out space—somewhere where you can close the door on the rest of the world, so it's good to make it a place that you really want to spend time in (and where your mates do too at sleepovers).

Redesign Your Bedroom

Step One: Research

Before you start, go to the library to get books on interior design or invest in a couple of magazines that specialise in bedrooms to give you ideas that you hadn't thought about. Work out how much money you can afford to spend and who might be able to help you with the time and labour.

Step Two: Clear Out the Clutter

Take a big bin bag and get rid of old books, scraps of paper, old magazines and clothes that you haven't worn for ages. See if anything is worth donating to a charity shop or can be recycled.

Step Three: Start Designing

Decide what look are you going for, then choose your color scheme accordingly. Remember that light colors open a room up and give a feeling of space whereas dark colors  can close it in and make it look smaller (but cosier). Most big DIY stores sell tiny sample pots now so that you can try colors out on your wall before your final choice. It's worth trying a few, as colors rarely look the same on the wall as they do on a color chart. Watch how the color changes at different times of day as the color you liked at noon may look totally different in the evening. Once you've decided, have confidence in your style choice. Some effects are:

- **Cool colors:** blue and green
- **Warm colors:** red, orange, yellow
- **Minimal:** white, shades of white or pale lilac
- **Bright:** vivid pink, orange, turquoise, lime green or yellow

- **Fairy tale:** pastel pink, pale blue, lilac, lavender or turquoise
- **Romantic:** shades of pink and red
- **Exotic** (Indian, Thai, Moroccan): honey gold, orange, yellow and reds
- **Stark:** black and white

Once you've decided on your colors, invite mates over for a painting party and it will be done in no time. Cover everything that might get paint splashed on it with old sheets or dust covers: i.e. the furniture, floor and yourselves!

Unless going for white all over, use a lighter shade of your wall color for the ceiling (or if you're going for something really bright and colorful, in which case, use contrasting colors). For doors, skirting boards and radiators, use a darker or lighter tone of the same color as the walls or a contrasting one.

If you want to use bold colors, but feel uncertain, the general rule is that opposite colors (red/green, blue/orange, yellow/purple) look great together and shades of the same color family look great together. Experiment on paper before hand to see how different color choices will look.

Step Four: Soft Furnishings

(e.g. curtains, blinds, bedspreads, cushions). It's always a good idea to get fabric samples before your final choice that way, you can see how the color looks in the room. Most fabric stores will give you a small strip from the end of a roll.

Don't mix too many contrasting patterns as they will all fight for space and give your room a confused look. When you add your pictures or posters, you want them to be the main focal point.

Here are some effects you might like to try:

- For a simple, uncluttered look, blinds at the window look clean and unimposing and if you keep your soft furnishing colors within the same color family as your walls, the whole effect will be easy on the eye, i.e. if you picked blue for the walls, choose soft furnishing in the same color group (pale blue, turquoise, sky blue, navy). If you chose green, the cushions and curtains should be in shades of green.

- For a bold bright look, go for contrasting soft furnishings. e.g. if you have blue walls, pick cushions in shades of yellow. If the walls are yellow, choose, cushions in shades of blue and purple.

- For a soft look, choose pastels and use fine muslin draped at the window.

- For an exotic look, choose spicy colors such as, red, orange and yellow. Drape sari material on a curtain rod over the window and have cushions made out of similar material for the bed.

- For a romantic look, have a canopy over your bed and use shades of pink and red.

Step Five: Lighting

Bedside and table lamps can make the room look soft and warm in the evening. Again, choose the color of your light shade to complement your color theme. Candles and night-lights can also be used to make the room look atmospheric in the evening (but be careful not to place them anywhere they can set fire to something!).

Step Six: Pictures and Posters

These are completely a matter of individual taste, but think about what you want to look at morning and night for the coming months or years. Pick the frames to complement your general look.

Step Seven: Personal Touches

Personal touches around the room will finish your look. Boxes to hold your jewellery, your favorite books, magazines, photos of friends. Save up for one fabulous piece—whether it be a jewelled mirror, some sort of nick-nack or a beaded cushion—and display it somewhere that will draw the eye.

Step Eight: Scent

Don't forget one of the most powerful senses, the sense of smell. Make your room smell wonderful with essential oils, room sprays or joss sticks.

Lucy's Room

I redecorated my room over a year ago when I realized that I had outgrown my girlie pink phase. I'd been into it in a big way and everything was P-I-N-K. I wanted something a bit more sophisticated so chucked out all my fluffy toys (except for my favorite teddy bear, Mr. Mackety—no way could I ever get rid of him. We've been through too much together). My room looks fab now. I spent ages trying out different colors and finally settled on lilac mist for the walls and a powdery, pale blue on the woodwork. Mum and I went down to Brick Lane in the East End of London and bought some gorgeous sky blue sari material with embroidered silver borders. We used it to make curtains and put a swathe of it over a curtain rail at the top of the window. That was the finishing touch and really brought the room together. The room looks soft and pretty now and I've started a craze for buying sari material for people's windows.

Izzie's Room

My bedroom has turquoise walls and I have deep-purple scatter cushions and curtains. I chose turquoise as it's supposed to be a healing color so I thought, what better choice for my personal space? I also like using scented candles so my room always smells lovely. At the moment, I have a mango one and it's divine. If I had my way, I'd like to build some sort of pyramid shape on the ceiling (like a pyramid shaped mosquito net!) as it's supposed to be a healing shape to lie to sit under, but Mum said no way, José. If I want to see the pyramids, she says I have to go to Egypt. Mum's an accountant and not big on creativity, which is why the rest of our house is cream, safe and immaculate.

Nesta's Room

Mum did my room. I trust her taste completely as she did a course in interior design and has a real flair for it. She chose a strong lavender for the walls and put pink muslin across the windows. My bed is like a princess's as it has the pink muslin draped from the ceiling down to the head. It looks romantic with all the muslin floating round it, but not too little girlie. I also have some red velvet heart-shaped cushions on the bed which look fab and are a good focal point for the eye. Plus, like Izzie, I like my room to smell gorgeous so I use exotic room sprays, like rose or lily.

TJ's Room

You have to be joking. My parents only know one paint color and that's magnolia. Boring and a half. My room looks really old-fashioned. It's even got patterned wallpaper—cream with pale green leaves on it. I hate it. Hopefully, next birthday they'll let me decorate and I'm going to go for all the Eastern colors. Deep orange, red and gold curtains and loads of exotic-colored scatter cushions so that it looks like a sultan's harem. Mum and Dad will probably have a heart attack.

Once you've got your bedroom sorted, here are a few fun things to do in there!

Find Your Pop Star and Your Romantic-Fiction Writer Name

For your pop star name, you take the name of your first female pet if you're a girl, male pet if you're a boy, then your mother's maiden name:

Izzie's: Zizi Malone

Lucy's: Smokey Kinsler

Nesta's: Sooty Costello

TJ's: Bubbles Bailey

For your romantic-fiction writer name, you take your middle name and the name of the street where you first lived.

Izzie's: Joanna Redington

Lucy's: Charlotte Leister

Nesta's: Suzanne Lindann

TJ's: Joanne Laurier

Quiz: Find Out What You're Really About!

1. Write down your three favorite animals in order of preference. Say why you've chosen them, e.g. cats because they're independent, penguins because they're funny, owls because they're wise.

   First choice reveals how you see yourself.
   Second choice reveals how others see you.
   Third choice reveals how you really are.

It's the adjectives chosen to say why the animal has been picked that are more revealing than the animal.

2. Make up your own book titles and authors. Here are TJ's favorites, for a start:

   Pusscat's Revenge by Claude Bottom
   Poo On the Wall by Hoo Flung Dung
   The Revelation of St. John by Armageddon Ottahere
   Bubbles In the Bath by Ivor Windybottom

Entertaining

Sleepover Special Report

Five Main Ingredients:

1. Nosh for the munchies and drinks
2. Videos/DVDs
3. Music
4. makeup
5. Mags

Izzie

Fave thing to do at sleepovers: Goss. Listen to music. Nosh.

Fave music for sleepover: World music, i.e. Arabic or Indian, so we can do a bit of exotic dancing.

Fave video: *Austin Powers: The Spy Who Shagged Me.* Yeah, baby, yeah!

Top nosh: Chocolate. Chocolate. And . . . chocolate.

Top drink: Organic elderflower juice.

Nesta

Fave thing to do at sleepovers: Dance. Read problem page in mags and have a good laugh. Makeovers.

Fave music for sleepover: Latest chill-out compilation, nothing too loud.

Fave video: Any horror. I love a good laugh, particularly when my wimps of mates hide behind the sofa.

Top nosh: Nettuno pizza with extra cheese. Häagen Dazs.

Top drink: Coke.

Lucy

Fave thing to do at sleepovers: Talk about boys and snogging, tell jokes (see some of my faves below).

Fave music for sleepover: I like getting out all my dad's old CDs from the late Sixties—then we can all do mad, hippie dancing. Something that Izzie particularly excels at.

Fave video: Any romantic comedy. I don't like violent or horror movies.

Top nosh: Chinese takeaway. Yum. Ben & Jerry's Chunky Monkey ice cream.

Top drink: Hot chocolate made with milk and marshmallows.

TJ

Fave thing to do at sleepovers: Chill. Laugh my head off. Get the girls to make up titles for my mad book collection (see page xx).

Fave music for sleepover: *Top of the Pops Summer CD* or anything we can dance to.

Fave video: An old favorite like a South Park Christmas Special, starring Mr. Hankey the Christmas Poo. Makes me laugh every time.

Top nosh: Burger and chips. Toffee popcorn.

Top drink: Banana milkshake with vanilla ice cream.

Sleepover Jokes

Lucy's Favorite Jokes

Q: What do you call a man with a wooden head?

A: Edwood.

Q: What do you call a man with two wooden heads?

A: Edwood Woodwood

Man goes to a doctor and says he thinks he's a dog.

"Have a seat on the couch," says the doctor

"I can't," says the man, "I'm not allowed on the furniture."

A man goes to a doctor and says he feels like a pair of curtains. "So pull yourself together," says the doctor.

TJ's Favorite Joke

Mahatma Ghandi, as you know, walked barefoot most of the time, which produced an impressive set of calluses on his feet. He also ate very little, which made him rather frail and with his odd diet, he suffered from bad breath. This made him . . . what? A super callused fragile mystic hexed by halitosis.

Dinner Parties

If you're planning something more sophisticated than a sleepover, like a dinner or lunch party, here are some tips from Nesta's mum:

Mrs. Williams's Tips for Dinner Parties

1. Keep it simple. Your guests are coming for the company so don't try and do something complicated to impress them or you'll end up harassed and in the kitchen with

no time to sit down and spend time with them.

2. Find out if anyone's vegetarian or has special dietary needs (like being a chocoholic).

3. Spend a little time making your table look good. It needn't cost a lot. If you're going to put flowers on the table, keep them low so that guests can still see each other. Colored napkins, candles, leaves, berries, ivy or flowers from the garden all can be used to make the table look special. (Check with your parents first, though, if using flowers from the garden, as you don't want to land yourself in it when they realize that you've used your mother's prize roses to impress some boy.)

4. If there's someone in particular you'd like to sit next to, do a seating plan so that it isn't left to chance and you get stuck with your brother. Also, a last minute, "Oh sit anywhere," means that a shy person may be put next to someone equally as shy, while all the extroverts are down the other end of the table having a jolly old time.

5. Have a trial food preparation run on a night before the dinner party so that you know exactly what to do and how the meal will turn out. Don't

try out new recipes on the night.

6. Choose a recipe where you can do most of the preparation beforehand (the day before is ideal so you have a whole day to make yourself look gorgeous for the dinner party) and just heat it up when guests arrive. That way, you can spend time with your guests.

7. Cheating is absolutely okay. If you've bought prepared food, take it out of its foil and knock the edges about a bit so that it looks homemade. Add your own herbs, cream, vegetables and croutons. Remove all traces of packaging from the kitchen. Add your own fruit, sauce or icing to desserts.

8. Give yourself time to get ready, well before anyone arrives.

Nesta's Tips for Dinner Parties

- Remember to turn on the oven.
- Read the labels on tubs in the freezer so that you don't serve

creamed cod as vanilla ice cream by mistake, like I did once.

- Try not to burn your hair or eyebrows when lighting candles, (Um, something that I also did!)
- On second thoughts, here's my best tip for dinner parties: Go out to eat!

Parties

If you're planning a party:

- Send out invites in plenty of time and ask guests to RSVP so that you know how many are coming and can organise food and drink. Be clear about the date and arrival time. Sometimes open-house parties mean that your guests arrive and leave in dribs and drabs. Best to start with a bang—everyone arrives more or less together and it's party time. You can lose the party atmosphere if it's a drop in invite and late guests may arrive to find plates of half-eaten food and weary hosts.

- Think about the music you want and make party compilations e.g. One chilled CD that makes good background music for when people arrive and are chatting and unwinding and one more upbeat one for later that will get everyone up and dancing. If you pick your music well, it will avoid guests interfering and going through your whole CD collection, leaving it all out all over the floor and putting CDs back in the wrong cases.

- Soft lighting can make rooms look atmospheric and

remember—everyone looks better by candlelight and nightlights really make a place look soft and welcoming.

- Scents are powerful mood enhancers. Room sprays, essential oils and scented joss sticks can all be used to create an aromatic experience. Try burning cinnamon and orange essential oil at Christmas; ylang-ylang, rose and sandalwood for a romantic scent and lime and bergamot in summer for a clean, light fragrance.

- Delegate. Don't try to do everything yourself. Get a few mates round early and ask them to help (you can also get dressed together and get into the party mood early). Ask one to greet guests and to take coats, another to make sure everyone's got a drink, another to pass round any snacks. It will give them a ready-made chance to chat and is a really good task to give to someone who is shy.

- Pay attention to all your guests, not just the ones you fancy. Introduce people to each other. They might all know you, but don't necessarily know each other.

- If anyone brings a gift, acknowledge it. Don't toss it aside into a pile. Make a note of who brought what so that you can thank them later.

- Don't make anyone feel bad if they have to leave early. Thank them for coming and let them go.

Themed parties can be great fun as everyone has to dress up, which usually puts everyone in a great party mood. Here are our fave ideas:

An A–Z of Party Themes

A: African, Aztec, animals, *Alice in Wonderland*, Adam and Eve, Arabian Nights.

B: Beatniks, black and white, *Beauty and the Beast*, all in blue, bad taste, blonde bombshells.

C: Cops and robbers, cowboys and Indians, Chinese, cartoon characters, come as you were (in a past life).

D: Devils and angels, doctors and nurses, Dickens' characters.

E: Egyptian, Elizabethian, Edwardian.

F: Fairies and goblins, fat, the Flintstones, flowers or fruit, fave fictional character.

G: Gods and goddesses, gangsters and molls, glamour, ghosts, gender swap (i.e. boys as girls and girls as boys), Goth.

H: Hollywood (dress for the Oscars), Hawaiian, horror, hats, heroes and heroines, Harry Potter, hippies, hats.

I: Idols, Indian.

J: Japanese.

K: Knights and damsels in distress.

L: Legends, lords and ladies.

M: Marx brothers, Mexican, monsters, masks, milkmaids and farmers, Mexican.

N: Nuns and priests.

O: Oriental.

P: Pyjamas, all in purple, policemen and -women, Pre-Raphaelite, punk.

Q: Queens and kings.

R: Rock stars, rock 'n' roll, all in red, Renaissance, Romans.

S: Sci-fi, *Star Trek*, all in silver, school uniforms, Shakespearean characters, superheroes.

T: Thunderbirds, toga, roaring twenties, teddy boys and girls, toddlers and teddies, toys.

U: Uniforms.

V: Vicars and tarts, Victorians.

W: Walt Disney characters, whore or holy, all in white, witches and warlocks.

Z: ZZzzzzz—attend in your nightwear.

If you don't have a lot of money to spend on costumes, the simpler the theme, the easier it is, e.g. all in blue, pyjamas, gender swap or everyone in hats. Try and find a music track appropriate for the theme, e.g. Egyptian music if going for an Egyptian theme, 1920s music if going for the roaring twenties theme.

Party games can be great ice-breakers and really get guests interacting. If any guests really hate games, give them something to do so that they don't feel like a party pooper, e.g. look after the music, look after the drinks or take photos of the rest of the guests making idiots of themselves.

Our Favorite Party Games

Lucy's: Pass the Parcel

This needs some preparation by the host.

1. Take the prize (box of chocs, CD or whatever) and wrap it about forty times. You can use old newspaper for this.
2. Write down about thirty forfeits. Get your mates to help you to think things up or see the list below for ideas. Fold each forfeit and put in a bowl.

3. When it comes to playing, ask everyone to sit in a circle and put the bowl of forfeits in the middle. Ask one guest to man the CD player and to play some music as the other guests begin to pass the parcel, each unwrapping a layer as they pass it around. The music should be stopped at random. Whoever has the parcel when the music stops has to pick a forfeit out of the bowl and do it.

4. When the music starts again, carry on passing, unwrapping and stopping when the music stops to do a forfeit until the parcel is unwrapped and all that is left one layer. Whoever unwraps that wins the prize.

Ideas for Forfeits

1. Find out who has the biggest feet.

2. Go round the circle and curtsey to each person.

3. Sing the National Anthem at the top of your voice.

4. Do the Highland fling.

5. Do an impersonation of a gorilla.

6. Kiss all the boys on the cheek.

7. Pick a partner and impersonate two Sumo wrestlers fighting.

8. Go round the circle and stare at each person for twenty seconds without laughing.

9. Submit to being tickled by everyone.

10. Do ten press-ups.

11. Pick a partner and do a slow dance.

12. Say this tongue twister really fast, twenty times: Yellow lorry, red lorry. If you get it wrong, you have to start again.

Izzie's: Egyptian Mummies

Ask one guest to do the music, starting and stopping at different intervals, i.e. sometimes after five seconds, sometimes after forty seconds. Mostly, though, ask your music person to give team players enough time to do what they have to for a short while.

1. Ask your guests to make two teams. Boys versus girls is good.

2. Pick one person from each team to be your mummy. Line the team up, and give the first in line the roll of toilet paper. You'll need a ton of white toilet paper for this. The mummy stands opposite the first in line.

3. When the music starts up, the first member of each team has to race to the mummy and start to bind them, using the toilet paper as a bandage. It is important when doing

the face to remember to leave space around the nose and mouth for your mummy to breathe!

4. The first team member wraps and bandages until the music stops. They then go to the back of the line. When the music starts again, the next in line goes forward to continue the bandaging.

5. The first team to wrap their mummy completely from head to toe is the winner. (This is harder than it sounds, as when the wrapping is done too fast of tight, the toilet paper breaks!)

TJ's: The Adverb Game

1. One person has to go out of the room until they're out of earshot.

2. Those left in the room have to decide on an adverb, e.g. lazily or dramatically or urgently. When they have decided on the word, they call the person outside back into the room.

3. All the guests have to act in the manner of the adverb and the guest who was outside has to guess what the adverb is. They can make it easier for themselves by asking someone to do something in the manner of the adverb, e.g. "Snog Lucy in the manner of the adverb". Or, "Comb your hair in the manner of the adverb" and so on. It can be hilari-

ous and a real challenge if the adverb is something like "intellectually"—like, how do you snog someone or comb your hair intellectually?

4. When the guest guesses the adverb, choose someone else to go out of the room.

The reason I like this game so much is that it's a great excuse to get people do mad things "in the manner of the adverb".

Nesta's: Musical Chairs

1. Get all the dining chairs and line them up in a row, or back to back if you have a lot. As in the other games, ask one guest to look after the music.

2. Ask guests to form a circle around the chairs.

3. When the music starts, everyone moves round the chairs clockwise. When the music stops, everyone must attempt to sit on a chair. Whoever is left without a chair is out.

4. Each time the music stops, one chair is taken away.

5. The music starts again and round the guests go. When the music stops, once again, guests must sit and whoever hasn't found a chair is out.

6. This continues until there are two guests and one chair left. Whoever sits on the chair first when the music stops is the winner.

Sometimes it's a good idea to have a referee for this game as a lot of shoving and pushing can happen when there are fewer and fewer chairs—an independent eye is needed to see who really did sit down first.

Everyone's: Spin the Bottle

This is still a favorite—although you have to be careful who you play it with or else you can end up snogging someone you really didn't want to! The game is simple: everyone sits in a circle. You spin the bottle and whoever it points at is the Snogger 1. Then you spin the bottle again and whoever the bottle points to this time, is their Snogger. They have to snog each other or else they are out.

Non-Alcoholic
Cocktails for Parties
(sometimes known as mocktails)

Don't try to do too many, as it can get chaotic. Instead, offer a choice of four or five.

St Clement's: Half orange juice, half bitter lemon.

Parson's Walk: Half orange juice, half ginger ale, slice of orange.

Cranberry Cooler: Cranberry, lime juice and soda.

Virgin Mary: Tomato juice, a dash of Worcester sauce, dash of Tabasco sauce, lime juice, salt, pepper. Serve with a stick of celery.

Transfusion: Grape juice, ginger ale, lime juice.

Miami Vice: Pineapple juice, cream of coconut, wedge of pineapple.

Christmas Cheer: Bottle red grape juice, two cinnamon sticks, half a bottle of rum flavouring, four fluid ounces of Earl Grey tea, one tablespoon honey, one tablespoon of dark muscovado sugar, one orange cut into quarters and studded with cloves, Put the ingredients into a pan. Bring almost to the boil, then turn down the heat to the lowest possible. Serve warm.

Izzie's Special: carton of pineapple juice, two bananas, generous handful of watercress. Blend together. (I know it sounds weird, but it is totally divine.)

How to Give Someone a Special Day

Birthdays or days of celebration can pass by in haze of disappointment or be a total blast. It's up to you, but we think that special occasions should be marked. You don't have to have millionaire parents who can afford limos, marquees in the garden, private caterers and designer presents to have a good time. It's people who make occasions special and mates can make or break other mates' birthdays. We've put our heads together and talked about our perfect day, and have compiled this list of how to give somebody a truly fabulous day and spoil them rotten. The ideas would be good for Mother's Day, special birthdays (like sixteenth, twenty-first or for if a mate is down and you want to make her know that you care. Everybody loves to be shown how much people care about them so here's how to make someone feel like a princess for a day.

1. Breakfast in bed. Take up a carefully laid tray with a little flower, a napkin, a tray

cloth and whatever is the recipient's fave
breakfast. Lay it all out really beautifully so
that it looks as if effort has been made.

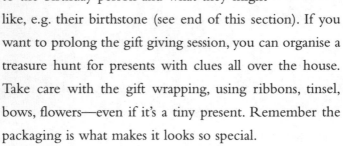

2. Cards and gifts can be taken up with the tray
   to be opened in bed. It's great if there are lots
   of gifts to open. Wrap everything—even silly
   things. Gifts needn't cost a lot, e.g. fave mag
   wrapped up, fave chewing gum, a key ring, a
   bar of favorite chocolate, a bar of favorite
   scented soap. Think about what is individual
   to the birthday person and what they might
   like, e.g. their birthstone (see end of this section). If you
   want to prolong the gift giving session, you can organise a
   treasure hunt for presents with clues all over the house.
   Take care with the gift wrapping, using ribbons, tinsel,
   bows, flowers—even if it's a tiny present. Remember the
   packaging is what makes it looks so special.

3. If you've no money, make a gift like a bracelet, a CD compilation or a photo frame with a silly or flattering photo of
   the birthday girl. Another idea is to go to an Internet
   astrology site that gives monthly horoscopes and print out
   your mate's for the next month. Anything that shows you
   have given some thought will be really appreciated.

4. At some point in the morning, have balloons or flowers delivered. This needn't be costly, as you can blow up balloons yourself and get a mate to deliver them.

5. Organise a pampering session. Club together with mates for a treatment or if you're broke, make a special voucher inviting them to a homemade beauty session with you and your mates as the beauticians. One of you can do a manicure or pedicure or a homemade facial.

6. Lunch. Either prepare a fave lunch or go out to a fave café with best mates. It can be as simple as cheese on toast, but it's still nice if someone does it for you.

7. In the afternoon, do a fave activity. Maybe a movie or bowling or if the birthday girl has any dosh to spend on clothes, book a session with a personal shopper.

8. Get friends together for a drink and birthday cake late in the afternoon. You could get sparklers for everyone to wave as you bring out the cake. If anyone is creative, ask them to ice the cake with a picture of something of interest to the birthday girl, e.g. a dress with designer logos for Lucy who's into fashion, or star sign symbols for Izzie.

Arrange phone calls from any long distance friends or fave relatives for this time.

9. Before evening activities, organise a luxury bath. Fill the bathroom with candles, pour in perfumed bubble bath and heat fluffy towels on the radiator.

10. If eating in, make the room look special so that when your birthday girl comes out of her bath, there's a terrific atmosphere to greet her. Get her favorite meal for the evening. It can be beans on toast or take away, if that's her favorite.

11. Invite friends round for a sleepover and get a fave movie.

12. Get together beforehand with mates and write a poem about the birthday girl. Put on a show and dress up in mad costumes to sing "Happy Birthday", e.g. get some willing boys to dress up as sugar plum fairies and dance round as they sing. Get someone from school who can sing opera to come and serenade her at the window. It will make the occasion especially memorable.

13. Have a last surprise under the pillow, even if it's a little chocolate or a tiny fluffy toy (if she's into them).

The secret to organising a special day is to arrange lots of enjoyable, entertaining and unexpected things and keep introducing them all day long. They needn't be expensive, but by the end of the day, your birthday girl will feel like a million dollars.

Birthstones

Some of your birthday girl gifts could be inspired by birthstones (or birthstone lookalikes) Here's a list of them:

January: Garnet (wine red)
February: Amethyst (purple/violet)
March: Aquamarine (bluish green)
April: Diamond (clear)
May: Emerald (green)
June: Pearl (off white)
July: Ruby (red)
August: Peridot (olive green)
September: Sapphire (blue)
October: Opal (milk white)
November: Topaz (yellow gold)
December: Turquoise (turquoise)

Holidays!

And so to holiday time. Hurrah. Time to chill out, relax and enjoy. But first you have to decide what to take!

The Essential Summer Holiday Wardrobe

- A flattering bikini or swimsuit. Take a friend with you when shopping for this for an honest opinion.

- A sarong for covering any lumps or bumps while you cruise past boys by the pool or on the beach. It can also be used as a shawl in the evening if it's cool.

- A practical beach bag, big enough to hold all your stuff. It's worth hunting around for one that zips shut so sand (or a pickpocket) doesn't get into it.

- A light floaty dress for evenings (short or long).

- T-shirts and light trousers in the same colors. Minimise the number of clothes you take to either, all white, all black or all blue and you can easily mix and match.

- A lightweight jacket for cool evenings.
- Pretty sandals or flip-flops.
- One pair of trainers or comfy shoes for trekking or sightseeing.
- A hat (straw, baseball cap or other) for when the sun is strong or your hair has gone mad.
- One special outfit for the evening, for if you meet a cutenik on the beach and get a date.
- One fab pair of sunglasses.

Some Other
Things You May Find Useful

- Camera, plenty of film and a back-up battery.
- Ear plugs for if your room is next to a boiler or if you have noisy people next door.
- Sun screen lotion and après-sun (v. important).
- Books and magazines.
- Hair ties for the pool or sea.
- An eye cover in case your room blasts with sunlight at five a.m. and wakes you up.
- Lip salve for dry lips.
- Eucalyptus oil for the plane. Germs get circulated through

the air in the cabin, and eucalyptus is antiviral, so if you sprinkle some on a tissue and inhale every now and then, it will help prevent you from picking up a cold or virus.

- A fan.
- Travel plug.
- Nail file.
- Hairdryer.

Tips for Taking Great Holiday Pics
by Steve Lovering

- Make sure you have plenty of the right kind of film and a back-up battery (or card if your camera's digital). Put it in your hand luggage, because checked luggage is X-rayed at a much greater strength since the advent of heightened security in airports. Sometimes it's worth buying a disposable camera—you can get ones that take panoramic shots and even work underwater which is great for pool and ocean shots.

- Check where your light source is. It is always best coming from the side or three quarter front as this avoids your shape casting a shadow over the picture.

- Take your pictures early in the morning or early in the evening when possible, as the light is best then, but make sure the light is in the right place or your subjects may become silhouettes. At high noon, the light is harsh and photos tend to come back with hard shadows under eyes and hats.

- Let your pictures tell the story of your holiday with a beginning, middle and end, i.e. packing before going, a

tearful goodbye to the dog, cruising at the airport, arriving at the hotel, the places you visit which reflect the culture, then finally arriving back to the angry dog who wasn't pleased he was left behind!

- Think about your composition. Look at what's around your subject—you don't want a photo where it looks like someone has a tree growing out of their head, or where the top part of their head has been cut off (unless it's a pic of my brother Lal—I always try to cut off his head).

- See if there are any colors around that will look good against your subject. For example, if someone's wearing a yellow dress, put them against a contrasting background like a purple flowering bush.

- Compose your subject so that they aren't looking straight into the sun and squinting.

- You don't have to force the subject to pose straight on. Try a three-quarter angle for example. If taking in the whole body be careful you don't cut off at strange points, making the subject look as if they have no neck or no lower leg (unless it's Lal again when care must be taken to make him look as ridiculous as possible on all occasions).

- Don't always have the subject dead centre either—try putting them a third of the way in.

- Look for lines in the landscape that may lead the eye to your subject, such as a row of hedges, or a wall.

- Beware of spilling water or drinks on cameras as it can cause damage that is expensive to repair and won't be covered by insurance.

PART FIVE
Riding the
Roller Coaster

by all of us

We all experience crapola days sometimes and periods when the outlook seems cloudy and we lose our usual fight or optimism. Sometimes it can feel like life is a roller coaster with ups and downs, highs and lows, good times and bad. Rejection, loss, illness, stress . . . they all cast a shadow and can make us feel the world's a hard place and that life's nothing but an uphill struggle and we may as well give up.

Trouble is, when in a down patch, it can seem like it's going to last forever, with no end in sight. At times like this, different people have different ways of coping or a favorite saying that inspires them and reminds them that there is light at the end of the tunnel and it's not an oncoming train!

This next section about how we cope with the down times, plus some of our favorite sayings—so when the going gets tough, the tough can turn to this section and hopefully find something to help.

Izzie

The girls asked me to go first because I'm known as the one who is always asking questions about life. In fact, the teachers at school call me Izzie "Why?" Foster because of my reputation for always asking difficult questions. My mum says I was always like that, even as a small child when my favorite questions were things like, "What's after space, Mum?" I never did get satisfactory answers and the questions still rattle away in my brain sometimes driving me mad.

The girls call me the "wise woman" because I'm always thinking about deep stuff. Wise woman is a joke. If they only knew how mad I was inside my head. Sometimes, it all gets to me—the bad news on TV, like people getting killed, wars, people with not enough to eat. I think, Why, why, why? It's sooo not right. None of it makes any sense. And then on a smaller, more personal scale, there's my own life. Boys, mates, family, exams, school, the size of my expanding bum. How do you cope and stay sane?

Well, of course there's chocolate for a quick fix, but it doesn't last for long (except on your hips!). And putting my feelings down as lyrics for my songs also helps, but I've tried to find something that gives a lift in the longer term (and isn't fattening!). As I said earlier in the book, I'm into aromatherapy—in fact, into all New-Age therapies. I find it really interesting how essential oils or crystals or a good massage can affect one's state of mind as well as the physical self. Out of all the things I've looked into, I've found that visualisations and meditation have helped me the most, as they calm me down and make me feel at peace. And if I feel peaceful inside, it is reflected outside. In life, I think that it's not what life throws at you that's so important, but how you respond to it. And that can all be down to the state of mind you're in at the time. If you feel chilled, then nothing seems such a big deal. If you're stressed, the smallest thing can blow your fuse.

Here are some techniques I've learned to help achieve a positive frame of mind. They're particularly good if you have exams coming up or are at the dentist's or, in fact, in any stressful situation.

Izzie's Visualisation Technique to Take Your Mind Off Bad Times

1. Lie back, close your eyes, uncross your legs and arms. Take three deep breaths, right down into your abdomen.

2. Think of a time when you were totally relaxed, confident and happy. Perhaps by a beach or a river or in the garden in summer.

3. Visualise the colors in your scene. Now turn them up, to make them brighter in your mind.

4. Imagine the sounds. Birds singing, leaves rustling or waves breaking on the shore. Turn the sounds up in your mind.

5. Imagine the smells. Fresh cut grass, the scent of roses or the salty air at the sea. Turn the scents up in your mind.

6. Bring all the sounds, scents and sights together into a complete picture in your mind.

7. Fix this picture with a physical sign. i.e. when you have the picture clear in your mind, make a gesture with your hands—either touch the thumb and index finger together or clench your fist. Every time you do this gesture in future, it will remind you of your

positive feelgood visualisation and take you to a cool state of mind quickly.

I read somewhere that it's not the bomb that's the problem, but the mind that created the bomb. In the same way, for example, think of a knife. You can use a knife to cut an orange or to harm someone. It's all down to the motivation that comes from inside, the knife is incidental. If the mind is peaceful, a person will feel peace and their actions will be peaceful. If a mind is agitated, a person will feel agitated and their actions will reflect that. I think that makes sense and I also think that meditation is one way of feeling peace inside. Imagine if everyone felt peaceful, what a fab planet this would be. Cue hippy-dippy song about love and peace. Everyone sing along . . .

There are loads of different types of meditation out there. It's worth researching a few methods to find the one that works for you, but here's one to try in the meantime.

Yoga Meditation

1. Sit comfortably with the spine straight.

2. Inhale and exhale through alternate nostrils. First put your right hand up to your face. Lightly rest your right thumb on the right side of your nose.

3. Rest your index finger on your forehead and have your middle finger ready by the left nostril for when you need it. The hand fits quite comfortably into this position.

4. When you are ready, apply a slight pressure with the thumb, closing the right nasal passage.

5. Now slowly inhale through the left nostril, hold for two counts, then apply gentle pressure on the left nostril with your middle finger (releasing your thumb from the right nostril as you do so) and exhale slowly through the right nostril.

6. Then, with the middle finger still resting on the left nostril, inhale through the right nostril, slowly; hold for two counts, then lift the middle finger from the left nostril and exhale through the left, closing the right nostril with your thumb again.

7. Try a few times to get the movements right, then do it slowly up to ten times.

8. Once you have mastered the technique, you can sit and do it for ten minutes or longer and it will bring about a sensation of calm and focus.

Did you hear about the Buddhist who refused painkillers during a root canal?
He wanted to transcend dental medication.

And here are a few of my favorite quotes. I have them stuck on the noticeboard above my desk in my bedroom to remind me.

What you resist, persists.

It's never too late to change.

The only time that's real is here and now.

You'll never learn to sing if you're not prepared to open your mouth and hit a few bum notes.

Some days you're the bug, some days the windscreen.

Eat, drink, and be merry, for tomorrow we diet.

We do not discover new lands without consentingto lose sight of the shore for a very long time.– André Gide

Dream as if you will live forever, live as if it's your last day.

A woman is like a tea bag. You don't know how strong she is until you put her in hot water.

If you tell the truth, then you don't have to remember anything.

Nesta

Okay, what cheers me up? Hhmmm. Twenty-five pounds in my pocket and permission to spend. I'm a great believer in retail therapy. When the going gets tough, the tough go shopping. It can take your mind off whatever's bugging you.

Now, that may make me sound like a shallow person, but I'm not really. I just don't believe in dwelling on bad times. I believe in getting on with life. There's that saying that life is what you make it and I intend to make mine fab. Like, why sit around in your room, moping over some guy when you can be out seeing a new movie or trying on shoes at the mall?

Yes, there have been times I've been dumped (yes, *moi!*) There was a time I was bullied at school (I wrote about this earlier in the surviving at school section), but I decided, I had a choice. Winner or loser? I chose winner. And I really *do* believe we have a choice.

Life is not a rehearsal. I mean, yeah, who knows how long we've got on the planet, why we're here and all that stuff? What we do know, though, is that we *are* here so why not see as much as you can, experience all that there is? I intend to make the most of it and be as happy as I can.

Here are my favorite quotes for the bad days:

Quitters never winand winners never quit.

No one can make you feel inferior without your permission.

People who refuse to hold out for anything,
but the best very often get it.

*Better one day as a tiger, than a thousand
as a sheep (Chinese proverb)*

*The birds of doom may fly overhead,
but you don't need to let them nest in your hair.*

You laugh because I'm different, I laugh because you're all the same.

Don't wait for your ship to come in, swim out to it.

Choice, not chance, determines destiny.

*If you have but two coins, buy a loaf for the body with one and
hyacinths for the soul with the other.*

If at first you don't succeed, then skydiving is not for you!

Coffee, chocolate, men. Some things are just better off rich.

*Don't upset me.
I'm running out of places to put the bodies.*

Lucy

My methods of getting through bad times are very simple:

1. Spend time with your mates, having a laugh.
2. Love the people close to you and be there for them in bad times and they'll do the same for you.

I know that there are loads of people on the planet who are having a really hard time, but what about people in the neighbourhood? My brother Lal (who is not normally known for his greatly compassionate nature) was really kind to this oddball old lady who lived nearby. And her cat. It really touched me because everyone else avoided her, but he took a little time with her. I thought afterwards, it's so easy to feel a great need to help people that we see on the news on the telly, and to overlook the ones who live in the same street who are lonely or sad. Lal also leaves out food for the neighbourhood fox. He got really concerned when the council introduced wheelie bins as that meant that the fox couldn't scavenge for food in the rubbish bags any more, so was going hungry. Lal now spends some of his money on food for the fox. He can be a real sweetie, sometimes.

3. When I'm feeling low, I love making clothes. I can spend hours looking in fabric stores, at jumble sales or stalls selling old clothes down the Portobello Market, looking for the perfect piece of velvet or lace or piece of material to make into something fab. It gives me a real buzz putting it all together and it always lifts my mood.

4. If dumped, allow twenty-four hours of wailing, listening to sad songs and feeling sorry for yourself. Then get up, turn the page and move on. (Chocolate, ice cream and weepie videos are also good in the first twenty-four hours.)

Here are my favorite quotes:

Fortune favors the brave.

What a difference a day makes, twenty-four little hours.

Big things come in small packages.

Two mistakes you can make in life: one is to think that you're special. The other is to think that you're not.

He who laughs, lasts.

Look for the rainbow in every storm.

Laugh and the world laughs with you.

The darkest hour is just before dawn (so if you're going to steal your neighbours milk, that's the time to do it!)

TJ

Low points? Oo. Er . . . Well, I know the one thing that doesn't work for me and that's lying around, thinking about it. That can feel like wading through a pan of cold porridge (not that I've ever waded through a pan of cold porridge, it would have to be a big pan, for starters, but you know what I mean!) When I'm feeling down—it might sound mad—but I jog or play squash, football or tennis. Thrash a ball about. It works. Honest. Like, there was this one time when I fell in love with a boy, *really* in love. Luke De Biasi. I thought he was my soul mate (but unfortunately he happened to be going out with Nesta at the time). Anyway, he really messed us both around, telling lies, telling half-truths, and at the end I felt so mad and confused, I didn't know what to do with myself. So I took myself off to the squash court, imagined he was the ball and bashed the hell out of it. Better than doing him physical damage and I felt a lot better after! Kind of purged and free. My mum's always saying that bad feelings are better out than in. I think she means that I should express them, like talk them through or something, but I prefer to do it this way. And I always feel better afterwards.

I keep a diary, just for me. I'd die if anyone ever saw it so

I keep it locked and hidden. I put everything in there—good, bad and indifferent. It helps. Just putting it down in words gets it out of my head.

To feel good, I also like to read. I feel like it expands my mind. There are all these different people on the planet. Sometimes, when going down the road I look at someone and think, what's your life like? What are you all about? What's *your* world? Reading lets me see into other people's lives and imaginations, so different from my own, and I get a real buzz out of that.

Best of all, though, when I'm feeling low I turn to my mates. I feel so lucky to have got in with Lucy, Izzie and Nesta. After my best friend, Hannah, left to live in South Africa in Year Nine, I felt so lonely and thought my life was over. They showed me that it wasn't, and that only a chapter had finished so that a new one could begin. They've been totally top. I would say that friends are the best remedy for low times. They can make you laugh, give you advice, see you through the times that don't make sense.

Here are my favorite quotes:

When spiders unite, they can tie up a lion. (Ethiopian proverb)

One loyal friend is worth a thousand relatives.

Friends listen to what you say.
Best friends listen to what you don't say.

Keep a diary and one day it'll keep you.

This above all: to thine own self be trueAnd it must follow,
as the night the day, Thou canst not then be false
to any man.Polonius, in Hamlet.

The longest journey starts with the first step.

He who would climb the ladder must begin at the bottom.

The road of life is always under construction.

If you want a friend, be a friend

Never test the water with both feet!

239

And finally, while we're talking quotes, we couldn't leave out old Confucius!

Confucius, he say: man with no front garden look forlornConfucius, he say: who say I say all those things they say I say?

And finally *finally*:

Everything is possible—except skiing through revolving doors.

Bye for Now!

Well that just about wraps it up, folks. That's all we've learned so far in our fifteen years/seven hundred and eighty weeks/five thousand four hundred and seventy-five days/one hundred and thirty-one thousand and four hundred hours (approximately!) on the planet. Hope you've enjoyed reading it as much as we enjoyed compiling it and you never know, we might be back when we're older and wiser with whatever we learn in the future. Watch this space!

Lots of luv,
Lucy, Izzie, Nesta, and TJ.

The books that all your mates have been talking about!

Collect all the books in the bestselling series by

Cathy Hopkins